The Eagle Feather : Life is Hard, but Beautiful Copy

The Eagle Feather Saga Book 1

A. K. Vyas

For Emilian and Louisa

In Loving Memory

Bret Ryan Sommers

1972-2004

The best and brightest are taken too soon.

I'll see you on the other side, brother.

"I was not the lion, but it fell to me to give the lion's roar."
-Sir Winston Churchill

Contents

Preface

Human nature is eternal. This is why we can relate to people we've never met across oceans of time, with different temperaments, talents, and convictions. Life expectancy in the Stone Age was only thirty-five short years. Yet they lived, loved, and imagined, just as we do now. Millenia from now, the trappings of life in the early 21st century may similarly be considered Hobbesian. Our future descendants will still need grit, dark humor, and the entrepreneurial spirit.

As a father, only now have I begun to comprehend the depth of love and responsibility that comes with the blessings of parenthood. Children are the future, and limitless in their potential. Civilization progresses in leaps and bounds. Somewhere, somehow there are little boys and girls out there who will use their imagination, courage, and entrepreneurial spirit to better the human condition.

My father, a retired US Army officer from the Vietnam War era, missed meeting his grandson by slightly over a year. He always taught me through stories which is the old way, the proven way. Afterwards, he would always ask questions and we'd discuss opinions as food for thought.

This story passes this tradition on to our little boy who is fascinated by dinosaurs, woolly mammoths, Sabretooth, and the great outdoors.

Perhaps it might also benefit other young people, or the young at heart.

CHAPTER ONE
THE SONG

"Knowledge is like a lion; it cannot be gently embraced."
-South African Proverb

THE DUSKY SMOOTH SNAKE slithered unseen down the verdant leafy branches toward the little boy.

Coal-black serpentine eyes hardened. Its inky forked tongue flickered out, tasting the balmy air.

An arid wind gust suppressed the menacing hiss, as the bigger boy began climbing.

The young boys of the Auroch People were hunting mottled bird eggs across the great silver-brown steppe. All but one. Emil lay under the lush, cool shade of a gnarled old tree. He was watching the shapes of the puffy white clouds overhead, imagining fierce shaggy mammoths, and his egg pouch was nearly empty. Dori came running to the tree with a full egg pouch. He gently added a few eggs to his best friend's pouch, then began climbing with a grin. "Emil, Emil, we are hunting eggs! Who cares about clouds?" Emil just smiled at his husky friend.

Emil was startled by a sudden painful scream as Dori fell to the ground with a thud. Emil looked up and saw the snake's scaled tail disappear into the high grass. Dori was pale with a glossy complexion and barely breathing. There were two large red bite marks on his neck. Emil pulled Dori away from the tree while screaming for help. As Papa had taught him, Emil took a sharp flint from his pouch. Tomi, one of the older boys, ran over. Emil gave him the flint in a daze. Tomi opened Dori's wounds and began sucking and spitting the venom out of the bite.

The rest of the boys came running over, as did Emil's mother Lulu. Dori was gone.

Emil stopped hugging his friend and walked off with bright watery eyes. Life was hard for the People. He didn't want them to see him cry.

Back near the village, Emil was absent-mindedly fetching water from the bubbly spring. He felt his mother's warm arms wrap around him. Lulu sang him a new song about Dori. The People were sure no one knew more songs than Lulu, not even the Elders.

Emil voiced softly, "Mama, it was all my fault, I should have been climbing the tree, it should have been me, and I cried too."

Lulu kissed her son on the forehead and then took his little face in her hands, while looking him in the eyes. "Life is hard, Emil. It was Dori's time. There's no fault here. We'll think of Dori tonight and honor him at the Spirit Ceremony. We can cry, then we go on." Emil hugged Mama tight.

Shouts of excitement rang through the camp at dusk. The men were returning from a successful hunt. The dusty hunters were tired and sanguine. Emil ran at full speed for Papa, Aash, jumping into his arms, and checking for wounds.

"I'm fine, Babo," grinned Papa, running a coarse hand through Emil's sandy brown hair. Papa gave Lulu a quick hug and kiss. Emil always insisted on carrying Papa's heavy spear when the hunters returned. "Babo" was what the People affectionately called their young boys.

Papa's charcoal ash spear was a source of pride for Emil. It was perfectly balanced, tapering into a conical obsidian spearpoint. Papa led a hunting team for the People. He was the only hunter in the village who made his own spears. Emil said, "Dori is gone." Papa knelt, then nodded while he held Emil's hand tight and gave him a big kiss.

Then he prompted quietly, "First the Daily Task." Emil nodded.

Life was hard for the Auroch People. They were nomadic hunters of the plains. Everyone had daily tasks and the order was important. The task order was village, tools, body. The

People had to be ready to move, hunt, or defend themselves on a moment's notice.

Everyone had camp jobs. The children set snares, hunted eggs, and gathered water and wood. The women worked the hardest. They maintained the fires, and gathered food while watching the children. They skillfully mended anything that needed it, and guarded the camp during the day. When the men weren't hunting or scouting, they were repairing the Ghers and weapons.

First, the village tasks. Fix Ghers, traps, snares, anything that needed repair. Second, equipment tasks. Each hunter would make sure his flint or obsidian-tipped spears were ready. The women would mend footpads before cooking the meat. The children's responsibility was water. Only then would each person see to their own needs. Finally, the People all relaxed together. It was time for joking, talking, and eating around the large roaring fires. This was the best part of the day.

Emil was cleaning the water pouches, when he heard light footsteps behind him. The boy spun around and grinned despite the grim events of the day. A sunny voice said, "You're good, little man, I usually sneak up on people. Your papa tells me you had a long day." It was Bret, who at seventeen winters wasn't the youngest hunter of the People, though he was the smallest hunter in the village.

Bret had briefly been on the same hunting team as Papa back when they were young hunters. The little hunter was always upbeat.

The People teased Bret. He was so easily underestimated when standing next to the towering Leif, or the powerful Bron. There was also the shaking. The village boys passed rumors that Bret's hands and knees often shook before and after hunts. They'd smirk about this behind his back. This was understandable from young boys who'd never missed a meal, or faced a charging Grizzly. Yet, many of the adults teased the little hunter as well.

Emil had seen the little hunter's hands shaking one foggy morning before hunting a cackle of marauding hyenas.

Bret had said, "It's true my hands can tremble before a hunt. If they knew where I was taking them today, they'd shake even more."

Emil knew Papa, who joked and playfully teased with everyone, truly respected the little hunter. The boy liked Bret because he was funny, and never talked down to him like he was a kid.

Emil told Bret about Dori. The little hunter squatted down on his haunches to face the boy.

"That's a rough day. A snakebite took my mother too, when I was a bit older than you. Snakes kill more people than any other forest creature, Emil. Always be alert for snakes. Now let's see your water pouch, young buck."

Bret looked it over; there was no design on it. Bret began carving a flying fish design into Emil's leather water pouch. "A flying fish has always been lucky for me on the hunt, so now you have one too. We actually make our own luck, Emil, but every bit helps."

Emil thanked him. The little hunter went on, "Do you want to learn a trick that helps me run fast?" Everyone knew Bret ran like the wind.

Bret told him, "If you are relaxed you can run faster and longer. Loosen up before runs. First, I want my arms relaxed, so I drop my arms and really shake my fingers. Then I make sure my jaws are stretched and loose."

Bret stopped and looked Emil in the eye. "At first whenever I was sad, I ran. Then just to do it. Now the wind itself can't catch me."

The little hunter shook his hand firmly, and walked off into the scarlet-orange sunset. The tantalizing smells of sizzling meat wafted over the village. Emil finished cleaning the water pouches just as Mama called him to eat.

Bret was quietly talking with Papa at the evening meal. His finger traced a slow, treacherous circling path around the village. Papa nodded and tested the wind. *He looks very serious*, thought Emil. Then Papa saw him watching, and scooped him up with a tickling hug.

Emil sat cuddled between his parents eating quietly. There was ripe fruit, mottled blue eggs, and plenty of fresh roasted meat from the day's hunt. Papa was very quiet afterwards, and Mama knew something was on his mind.

Later in their Gher, Papa told Emil, "Crying isn't weakness, but don't do it too much. Dori was a good boy who died finding food for the People. He's made the journey we must all make. Dori's with the Sky Spirits of our ancestors now, little one."

"You cry too, Papa?" Emil asked.

Papa nodded and said, "Life is hard, Babo, but beautiful. Everyone cries sometimes. Then we must be brave and go on."

As Emil slept, Mama held Papa close. "I worry for him, he blames himself for poor Dori, and the others tease him for daydreaming," she said.

Papa smiled. "I was never the strongest boy or the fastest, and the best girl in the village picked me. Emil never quits. His mind is swift, and he speaks the truth with a smile or rhyme. The People will respect this."

Then Papa whispered, "There are fresh Sabretooth tracks circling the village. This will be trouble. Keep yourself and the boys close to the village for now." Papa held Mama's head snug to his chest until she fell asleep.

Emil woke up to Mama's cheerful blue eyes and smiling face. Papa and Mama's sleeping furs were neatly rolled and tied. Mama told Emil, "Babo, make your sleeping furs, have some water, and then go check the little traps with the boys."

Emil was still sleepy, asking, "Mama why do we make the sleeping furs first every morning?"

Mama said, "It's our way. When the first thing we do in the morning is make our sleeping furs, we start the day doing something right. Some days are good, others are bad. This way, every day starts with something we can control and do right."

As Emil was making his sleeping furs Mama said, "Papa and the hunters want everyone back in the village before dusk. After morning chores there will be a fire lesson."

Fire was very important to the Auroch People. It kept them warm, cooked their meat, and kept them safe at night. Everyone in the village must know how to quickly make fire with sticks, moss, or flint.

The sound of singing in the camp welcomed the hunters' weary return at dusk. Emil ran to Papa, boisterously singing a new song.

"First a dry stick long
Then flat wood wide
Turn it fast with song
Until sparks inside
Then tinder slow
Blow, Blow, Blow!"

The dust-covered men sipped water and hugged their families in greeting. All the children were scampering around like happy little monkeys. They were singing this new song with glee.

Papa scooped up Emil and sat him up on his shoulders. *Children are so resilient*, he thought. Mama hugged Papa with a proud smile on her face. "My son Emil made up a fire song and all the children use it to remember."

Papa's dark brown eyes wrinkled in reply. "Oh, you mean my son Emil has a new fire song for the People. You must teach me the words."

Emil looked down. "Papa, is there fresh meat today?"

Papa shook his head. "We chased a herd of red deer all day into the hills, and speared a big one. It passed right by the cave of a great bear as it died. He took our kill."

Emil said, "That's not right, it was our kill!"

Mama and Papa smiled and Emil already knew what they'd say.

"I know, I know, life isn't fair," Emil said.

Emil was curious: "Papa, was it a black bear or a Grizzly?"

Papa answered, "A big brown bear, and mean too. We wouldn't have let a black bear take our kill. With a Grizzly it's different."

Mama said pleasantly, "We gathered fresh roots, berries, and eggs today. There's enough food."

Lulu's cheerful spirit always warmed Aash's heart. Even if he didn't say this enough.

Papa looked up at Emil and whispered in his ear. "Learn from Mama, little one. Do you see how strong and cheerful she is? Life is hard, but beautiful."

Then it was time for the daily tasks. Emil and the boys ran off to clean water pouches and snag kindling for the evening meal. The sight of four little boys, wrestling a long thick log over to the fires, brought a smile to the hunters' weathered faces.

Papa was sharpening his obsidian spearpoint when he saw Emil do something curious. The boy stood alone shaking his fingers and loosening his jaw up and down, back and forth.

Then he watched Emil running laps around the village, as the other boys wrestled and practiced throwing spears. Mama called them both for the evening meal.

It was a beautiful summer sunset. This was big sky country. A blend of gently rolling white clouds with subtle purplish pink hues, all set amidst a backdrop of warm amber rays.

The evening fires cackled, jumped, and danced in the nocturnal winds. This was an invitation from the Sky Spirits to do the same. The rhythmic beat of the drums built up with sounds of laughter.

It would start with the children. As the drums clapped, they'd pretend to be the wavy flames themselves. Everyone knew there was fire in the body. Why else does smoke escape with breath in the cold? The women would join next. Everyone is young when dancing, waving their hands overhead, and laughing with little ones.

The men danced last, circling the flames with spears in hand. It was more jumping than dancing. Each man jumped up as high as he could to the beat of the drums. The running joke was the bravest men were actually the poorest jumpers. They jumped to thank the Sky Spirits for this day and for the company of brave men. They danced to renew their courage. It didn't matter if this worked or not. Every morning the hunters set out to face deadly hoofs, horns, and claws. The dangers of dawn were inevitable. The hunters had to produce meat for the People.

The children suddenly squealed with peals of laughter. Bret was doing his turtle dance. The little hunter would hop on one foot, then do a jumping spin, hopping on the other. Then he'd flop on his back with his arms and legs flaying like an upended turtle. The impressive part was the little hunter could flip off his back right back up onto one leg. As the children copied him, none of the People could keep a straight face. There is no sound in the world like happy children.

Papa stopped jumping and took over some drums to let the drummers dance. Emil settled in his lap, slowly adding the wild patter of little hands to the merry din.

"Papa," asked Emil, "Bret was on a hunting team. Why did he leave to hunt alone?"

Papa stopped drumming, declaring, "I don't know, Babo." Emil didn't like this answer.

Aash reminded his son, "A man's mind is his own until he cares to reveal it."

The boy thought this over carefully. Emil went back to playing the drums.

Chapter Two
Wolf Cub

THE WILY OLD SABRETOOTH struck that Stygian night. Even the owls were silent, as the moonless winds masked the big cat's presence until dawn. Tarik, the venerable old Spearmaker of almost thirty-four winters, was gone. From the tracks, he was taken as he stepped outside his Gher to make water. This was a severe blow to the People. Tarik's expertly crafted spears were vital for hunting and defense.

Papa quietly sifted a bit of dirt through his hand. His hunting team grimly prepared to track down the Sabretooth. Sev, the Chief of the Auroch People, inspected Papa's obsidian-tipped spear.

"Aash, you will not go hunt this Sabretooth," Chief Sev said.

Papa was confused. "Chief, we must avenge Tarik and kill this cat before it strikes us again."

The Chief nodded in agreement. "Yes, we will, but you are the People's Spearmaker now. You will hunt no more and fight only in defense of the village. Who should lead your team?"

They locked eyes in silence, then Chief Sev repeated softly, "Aash, ...who gets your team?"

"Bron," replied Aash.

Chief Sev gave final instructions to Bron, then put his hand on Papa's shoulder. "I, for one, value knowing a good man of twenty-three winters will be in the village when the hunters are away."

Bron clasped forearms warmly with Aash in gratitude, as the new Spearmaker said, "Blue skies, brother. Good hunting."

Aash gritted his teeth in silence as his hunting team left after the Sabretooth.

For the first time Emil could remember, Papa was there in the morning when he woke up. Bret was now also ordered to guard the village.

Mama hugged Papa close and whispered in his ear, "You are a great hunter, see this as an honor. Only you can do this for the People now. If our spears fail us, the village dies."

Emil just merrily grabbed his Papa's leg, declaring, "Now you can teach me to wrestle, hunt, and track, and make spears!"

Aash looked into his son's dark brown eyes. Emil shared his Opa's eyes. For the first time that dreary morning, Papa smiled. Seeing a young version of a lost parent will do this.

A maneater like this Sabretooth wasn't a normal predator which generally killed for food or if threatened. Maneaters can develop a fiendish taste for blood and begin killing for pleasure. Maneaters at first strike only at night, then grow bolder. Papa knew the People would need better weapons now, and fast.

After the morning tasks, Papa began inspecting the old Spearmaker's coarse dry stalks. The People preferred obsidian or flint for their spearpoints. Every hunter had a heavy ash spear balanced for his size and strength. The women and children needed weapons as well.

Emil was so excited watching Papa that morning. He sat imagining being a Spearmaker himself and was late for fetching the morning water. The People let boys gather eggs and water upon reaching six winters. The youngsters would boisterously joke, splash, and race the whole time.

To his surprise, Mama took his leather water pouch away, saying, "Emil, you were late. All the boys already left. You will not fetch water with the boys today."

Emil asked, "But why, Mama?"

Mama said, "You can never be late. We have to be able to depend on each other, especially when there is a maneater."

Emil pleaded, "But Mama, I can still catch them, and ...."

Mama interrupted, "If you're late on small things, you'll be late someday when it's important. You won't be there when your friends, hunting team, or the village needs you. This good habit starts with never being late. Are we clear?"

Emil knew Mama's stern voice. He uttered, "Yes, Mama," then he took Papa some fresh blueberries.

Papa smiled. "Thank you, Babo. Shouldn't you be fetching water with the boys?"

Emil looked down, confessing, "I was late, Papa. Mama said no."

"Ah," voiced Papa, "I see. The People cannot be late, Emil. Do you want to be a great woolly mammoth hunter someday?"

Emil proclaimed, "Oh yes, Papa, I want to lead a hunting team just like you!"

Papa remarked, "Then you can never be late. Lives depend on this. Mammoth or big-horned bison are large, powerful, and dangerous. Half the hunting team draws their attention, while the other half attacks from the rear. If either side is late, it can be very bad. Emil, almost everything is easier when you are a little bit early. Do you understand, Babo?"

Then Papa added with a wink, "We need to find more straight dry stalks for spears today. You can tag along."

Emil and Papa told Mama where they were going, then hiked into a dense, dark wooded area. The fiery sun had peaked for the day. They saw no animals and Emil asked, "Why?"

Papa explained, "It's too hot to hunt now, Babo. The animals are smart enough to know this."

Ironically, they instantly heard savage growls in the dense bushes lying just across the meadow. Papa grabbed Emil and quickly climbed a big oak tree.

Papa told Emil, "We're safe here."

A giant brown bear was fighting a pair of white wolves beyond the thorny foliage. The gnashing sounds of a fierce struggle resonated below. They heard a bear's triumphant barks and gurgling grunts fading away. The forest went completely silent.

Papa held Emil's hand tight, observing, "A great bear was fighting wolves. I think it's safe now. You stay up here in the tree until I come back. Mama and the People know we are here. Yes?"

Emil nodded. "Yes, Papa, I will stay in the tree."

Papa gave Emil a peck on the cheek. He climbed down the tree with his heavy spear at the ready. The bear had killed both wolves. The bear was gone. Papa called Emil down from the tree. *There must be very small cubs close by*, thought Aash. *This is the only reason a pair of wolves would be desperate enough to take on a Grizzly.*

"The Grizzly came for berries by the wolves' den," explained Papa. Sure enough, a small whimper emanated from behind a rock under a clump of sharp thorns. Papa reached in and pulled out a tiny fluffy white wolf cub.

Emil frowned. "The baby wolf is all alone now, Papa." He picked it up. The blue-eyed wolf pup was crying softly and immediately began licking Emil's face.

Papa proclaimed, "Put it down, Emil. I will give it mercy, then we go home."

He raised his war club. The orphan cub faced starvation or worse.

Emil started crying as well, pleading, "Papa, please! Let's take him, please, he's alone now!"

Papa thought, *This is silly. It's getting late and there's a maneater. We need to get back before dusk.*

Emil was carrying the sleeping cub in his arms as they returned to the village.

Back in their Gher, Emil was tired from the day. He fell asleep quickly with the cub cuddled in his arms. Papa went to remove the pup when Mama said, "No."

Papa knew this look and tone. Wise husbands know better than to test it.

The People did not understand saving the wolf cub. This was not the custom. It was yet another mouth to feed, and would someday be a large, savage wolf. Papa told the People the little white cub would eat only from his share, and there was peace.

Meanwhile, the People's hunters had tracked the Sabretooth to the edge of the Mountain River. It had crossed over into the realm of the Mountain Men. This was a dangerous warlike tribe it was best not to provoke. Many moon cycles passed with nary a sign of the Sabretooth. The game animals eventually returned. Bret went back to hunting.

Emil named the white wolf cub Cloud, and it became his constant shadow. The crisp spring turned into late summer, and then early autumn. Anywhere Emil went, Cloud would follow. As it turned out, Cloud actually helped bring in food. When the boys would hunt eggs, sometimes Emil brought a small bird or hare which Cloud had caught. Then one dark stormy night, Cloud became a true member of the People.

The wind was screeching wickedly on yet another starless new moon. Mama was leaving the Gher to make water when Cloud began growling aggressively. Papa sleepily grabbed his club to protect Mama. He noticed Cloud was growling at something just outside the Gher. Papa put Mama and Emil behind him and grabbed his spear. Cloud stopped growling.

In the morning, Papa saw fresh Sabretooth tracks just outside the Gher. The Sabretooth had been lurking this close during the night. It would have taken Mama. Papa went stark pale at the thought of this. For the first time, he picked up Cloud and gave the white wolf a fresh piece of meat.

The People's hunters once again tracked the big cat to the limits of the Mountain River. Chief Sev called a tribe meeting.

"Emil's wolf saved Lulu yesterday. It's one of us now. We'll find more such cubs when possible. This Sabretooth has a taste for man flesh. It'll become worse. I think this cat knows we stop chasing at the river. No choice—we'd lose even more lives in another war. It wouldn't surprise me if this Shaitan hunts both us and the Mountain Men back and forth."

Emil quietly announced to no one in particular, "We should talk to the Mountain Men and hunt it together."

Everyone laughed at this child's idea, except for Emil's parents and Chief Sev. *Talk to the Mountain Men? Ridiculous—they are mindless, bloodthirsty savages!*

The People, however, now saw how useful Cloud was. The white wolf helped in so many ways. His keen nose detected both predators and prey long before anyone else. The children gathering eggs or fetching water were much safer with Cloud around. The white wolf was dedicated to Emil, could run like the wind, and never tired. Papa thought, *The wolf can someday help the hunters run down prey they could never catch before. Cloud also keeps predators away from the village at night.*

The Auroch People, many winters from now, would eventually have dozens of wolf dogs in the village. The wolf dogs made a hard life easier. All of this was possible because of compassion. A little boy wanted to save a small white wolf cub that was scared and all alone in the world.

Chapter Three
The White Bison

"Where the cattle stand together, the lion lies down hungry."
-Maasai Proverb

A BLOOD RED DAWN started the day.

Snakes.

Of course, it has to be a snake. I hate snakes, thought the little hunter. The shaggy little bison was sprawled on all fours, silently crawling toward the herd. The chunky viper slithered through the heavy grass of the maize plains. The serpent's forked tongue smelled something odd about this little bison. Bison were dangerous. Their hooves were sharp with few blood vessels below the joints of their front legs. Deadly viper venom has to get into the bloodstream to kill anything.

The little bison froze perfectly still. It held its breath in silence. The naked sun's scorching glare punished everything under the heavens. Bret's sweat under the stifling hot bison skin had turned ice cold. The mercurial viper paused on a rock just paces in front of his face. They were eye to eye. Bret stared into those cold dead eyes, wondering if this was also the last thing his mother had seen

Only a fool would still be here, thought Bret. However, any sudden movement, even one in bison skins, could spook the herd. *Bison are dumb, but not that dumb*, thought Bret. The bison herd was almost in perfect ambush position. The People had carefully prepared this site. Bret saw the Old White Bull snorting in the lead.

The Old White Bull was legendary for his belligerent ferocity. Over the seasons, no fewer than three of the People's hunters had fallen under his hoofs and horns. The herd was on a narrow grassy ridge with a huge cliff. Everything was set. The People's hunting teams had lined the grassy area with animal grease in a semicircle around the cliff. As the herd passed, they'd torch the tall, straw-colored grass. The sudden smoky crescent of blazing fire should panic the trapped herd. The only clear direction left was over the great cliff. That was the plan.

The irritated viper decided to move on. Bret's heart started again as the last vestiges of its tail disappeared through the tall grass. The little hunter darkly pondered: *How many more vipers are out here? It's perfect snake country. The sun is scalding and there are rocky rodent holes everywhere.*

The lead bison were in the kill zone. Bret triggered the ambush by igniting the greased grass in front of him. The little hunter leapt to his feet screaming like a banshee as the fire took effect. At this signal, a full howling hunting team sprang up out of the grass lighting up the crescent.

The bison were terrified by the sudden smoke and fire. The herd fell over itself in panic. With a deep rumble, they slowly began thundering for the cliff's edge. Then the crafty Old White Bull saw a gap in the flames and turned for it. The entire herd swiftly followed suit.

A single young hunter hadn't lit his section of grass. The terrified bison herd tore through this gap, stampeding anything in their path. There was no escaping them. They were an irresistible flood of grunting hoofs and horns.

Bret saw Red gored into the air by a massive pair of gleaming white horns. When the redheaded hunter hit the ground, he was flayed apart, screaming. Dozens of deadly stampeding hooves rendered him a hazy pinkish mist. The panicked herd scattered in every direction as it cleared the searing flames. It was scorched chaos.

Two otherwise brave hunters lost their nerve seeing Red's fate. They dropped their spears and futilely tried to outrun the danger. Both were irresistibly swept under this thundering dusky tide. A thick dust cloud swirled into the heavens with the blistering smoke.

The Old White Bull charged the little hunter in full bovine fury. Bret's light spear barely nicked the charging beast. The little hunter instinctively dove forward as high as possible. Somehow, the flying leap completely hurdled the barreling bull. Bret landed awkwardly on his forearms with a painful groan. He looked up to see several bison thundering down upon him. The snorting white bison wheeled back to finish Bret. The little hunter was dazed and confused.

Dak saw Bret's miraculous flying dive over the Old White Bull.

Dak led this hunting team. A powerful man who, it must be said, always led his team from the front. Sometimes none of this matters.

Brave, Dak surely was…and stone-cold dead he was about to be. Dak shouted out the People's war cry, dashing to save Bret. The Old White Bull spun to face him. The bull's charcoal-red eyes burned with smokey fury.

Dak's heavy spear clanged harmlessly off the thick boss of the great bison's horns. The Old White Bull hooked his left horn from below. It caught Dak in the groin, completely eviscerating the shocked hunter. His wet innards slipped through the tears in his dusty leather shirt onto the dry grass below. Dak's eyes watered in shocked disbelief. He desperately tried to hold his insides together. Bret, as if in a nightmare, saw Dak's slippery fleshy coils slithering at his feet like bloody snakes. This was no dream.

Dak, the gallant team leader, slipped to his knees. The men locked eyes an instant before the great bison whirled back with an angry grunt. It stomped Dak into a gory, crimson pulp. The Old White Bull bellowed away in triumph. His ivory hide splattered with the brave hunter's ruby lifeblood.

The frantic bison herd stampeded past the little hunter. Bret could only lie prone, covering his head with his arms. His horrified screams were drowned out by the din of taurine grunts and the rambling of powerful hooves. The dust settled.

Then it was over. There was no sound save the still roaring sheets of cackling flame. Bret coughed in the merciful silence of thick smoky air. He thought, *Why am I alive?* It might have been luck. Perhaps it was because he'd forgotten to throw off his shaggy bison skins in the excitement. *It doesn't matter. There's no one else.* Nary a bison was in sight. A thick fleeting dust cloud on the horizon bore the sole remnant of their presence.

The entire hunting team had been wiped out. A heavy spear isn't much help against a terrified bison herd up close. Bret staggered from hunter to hunter. All five had been thoroughly gored and trampled. *There isn't much left of them. I'll save Dak's bear claw necklace for his family.* Bret salvaged a heavy spear and a few knives. He swallowed the hard lump in his throat.

"Thank you, brother," Bret whispered to the general area that had been Dak.

The little hunter covered his mouth from the thick smoke. He approached Zig's body despite the reticent heat from the blazing flames. *Why hadn't Zig lit his part of the grass?* Bret rolled what was left of Zig over. He squatted, squinting his eyes from the harsh heat.

Zig had been the youngest hunter on the team. *His skin is too red*, thought the little hunter. *Zig's water pouch is stark dry. It hasn't been filled today.* Bret thought back to morning inspection. He'd seen the young hunter bent over, retching. *Nerves*, Bret had thought. *The youngest hunter on a team is responsible for drawing water for the team.*

He pieced it all together. The team had run hard half the day in this heat to the ambush site. Dak had sagely made his team drink half their water before the final stalk.

Zig's skull was caved in by a great bison hoof, but at least he hadn't felt it. That explains it, thought Bret. *First, Zig had been sick. Then, he was late for inspection and had hastily filled everyone's water pouch but his own. Zig had no water. No one knew this. Of course, we'd have shared water with him. Zig's pride kept him silent. The sun, blistering heat, and strain of the stalk did the rest. Tardiness and pride.*

Zig was late and had made the second mistake. The People don't drill these lessons into the little ones for nothing. This is why I hunt alone, thought Bret.

The little hunter sadly shook his head. *It doesn't matter now*. Bret ambled over to the edge of the cliff. He cautiously peered over.

Not one. Not a single bison panicked off the cliff. No meat. This is disaster. All of this because of a single empty water pouch! The circling vultures will bring hyenas soon. I have to move.

Bret made his way down the ridge. His silhouette was framed dark and solitary on the harshly flaming horizon. Bret paused to check his direction. The sun, trees, and wind told him he was walking the wrong way in his stupor.

Bret fought the fog in his head. His dull headache was throbbing. *I'm not thinking straight. It's too hot. There's no shade anywhere on the plains. I need to cool off, there's barely enough water to make it back.*

Then his training kicked in. He could almost hear the Eagle Feather's voice in his mind's eye. Bret peeled off his shirt and peed on it. The little hunter wrapped the soaking shirt around his head. This instantly cooled his temples and refreshed his senses. Bret stumbled to a knee. He used a stick, a rock, and a shadow to pinpoint east. The lonely little hunter turned and trekked home alone.

Cloud sensed the little hunter before they saw him. Papa and Chief Sev saw the slight form limping solo out of the trees. Bret was covered in soot and scratched up by thorns.

Both men could see it in his eyes. This was the harsh reality of hunting big game with spear and club. The Spearmaker handed him a cool, leather water pouch. The little hunter took it but couldn't open it. His hands were shaking. Chief Sev gently took the pouch and opened it. Bret took a long, slow drink and emptied the rest over his head.

"Bad day," Bret said in a shaky voice.

Aash and the Chief nodded in patient silence. The little hunter threw the empty water pouch down. His usual sprightly eyes were resigned.

"They're all gone. Dak's whole team. The herd tore us apart," Bret said in a hollow voice.

Aash put his arm on the little hunter's shoulder. Bret looked down at the ground then handed him Zig's unused water pouch. The little hunter went on in a tired old voice.

"We were in perfect position. The herd walked right into the kill zone. We lit the ambush. All except Zig. I think the heat got him during the stalk. His section of the line wasn't lit. The Old White Bull headed for this gap instead of the cliff. They stampeded all over us. No place to run. There's nothing left of them. We didn't even get a single spear in one. Dak saved me. One hot day. Five brave hunters. A herd of bison."

Life was hard for the People.

Aash wordlessly felt the stark dryness of Zig's water pouch. He handed it to the Chief. Both men quickly figured it out, just as Bret had.

"Get some rest, Bret. I'll send a team out for them before the Spirit Ceremony," Chief Sev said.

Bret limped away in dejected silence. *This is the hunter's code. All for one. One for all. No man was left behind. No matter what. Living or dead. Your brothers would bring you home.*

Emil saw Bret and grinned innocently. He ran over to his limping friend, checking for wounds.

"I have some fresh berries, Bret!" said the boy joyfully. Emil set aside a hare Cloud had caught and retrieved for him.

The little hunter's hands had stopped shaking. He graciously accepted the berry pouch and sat silently on a log. As a rule, days like this were never discussed outside the circle of hunters.

Emil chirped away about his day. The boy described the races that day. He told Bret about the great new berry bush they'd found. Emil described a new wrestling move he wanted to try on Kilan. Bret wordlessly forced down a few berries with a listless look at Cloud's catch.

The little hunter's tired eyes crinkled at Emil's oblivious chipper chattering. The boy told his friend a silly old joke about finding a worm in an apple. Emil hugged the little hunter and ran off to play. Bret smiled despite himself. He thanked Emil silently and went to rest.

This was the answer. This is why we do it, Bret decided. *The little ones are worth days like this. We're here to protect them, but they keep us safe too.*

Emil ran over to Papa. The Spearmaker was repairing a shaky spear wrapping.

"When I'm a hunter, Papa, I want Cloud on my team!" Emil said. "He caught us a hare today! Papa, I think Bret is sad. What happened today?"

Papa answered, "Tough day, Babo. We lost a hunting team to the bison."

"All of them?" Emil asked incredulously.

Papa responded quietly, "Some days you get the bear, and some days the bear gets you."

The day's events spread darkly across the village. Anger and disbelief at the loss of an entire hunting team sparked strong emotion and calls for scrutiny. The evening meal was too quiet. By dawn, the village was seething.

Bron, the strongest hunter of the People, and Zig's big brother called for an immediate hunters' council that morning. They met in Chief Sev's Gher. A noticeably dejected Bret solemnly recounted the hunt's details. The Chief began talk of the Spirit Ceremony for the fallen, when Bron stood up with a derisive snort, and turned to leave the Gher.

Chief Sev commanded, "Bron, if you need to say something, say it now, in the open for all of your brother hunters to hear."

Bron said it harshly.

"This makes no sense to me. An entire hunting team? Dak was too good, and my brother, well I trained him myself... he'd never make this mistake. Why is it only Bret survives? The one responsible for initiating the ambush. He's not even on a hunting team. And well…we know he fears the hunt. I'm thinking it was not Zig's mistake."

Bret stood, reaching for his dagger. Cowardice was the supreme insult for a hunter, followed closely by lying. The little hunter's voice had a hard edge. "Bron, you talk the talk, do you walk the walk? Prove it."

Bron laughed contemptuously. "Hunters don't fight children, little man. Maybe the Spearmaker needs an assistant. You're no hunter, we all know this."

Chief Sev dressed down the room in a commanding tone. "Both of you idiots stand down. We've just lost five hunters! Five! Now two more of my hunters want to kill each other? Bron, you are way out of line here. Zig's water pouch had never been filled, mistake one. Then the second mistake was a tragic one: he was too proud. It's just as Bret said. The Spearmaker saw this clearly as well." *Everyone trusts Aash*, thought Chief Sev. *He'll defuse this nonsense.*

All eyes turned to Aash. He responded in a calm, even voice.

"It's true. Zig's water pouch was never filled. Zig was a good man, and my heart aches for your family, Bron. You couldn't be more wrong here, though, brother. Bret did his duty. Mighty Bron, you were an excellent second spear to me. Think this through. Like a team leader must…"

Bron's dismissive look cut through the Spearmaker's pacifying words. He turned, disgruntled, to leave again.

Aash's voice ratcheted into command tone, stopping Bron in midstep.

"Bron, one more thing. We all fear the hunt. We've all seen what's out there. Anyone who says different is a fool. Bret does his duty as well as anyone here. He consistently makes meat. It's your right to challenge Bret, and his to demand satisfaction. This bad blood will be pure disaster for your family. This isn't wrestling, Bron. Bret will end you. Of this I'm sure...and if he doesn't today... I will tomorrow."

The entire Gher was shocked by this final statement.

Bron turned back to Aash incredulously. "You take his side over mine, brother, after everything we've hunted together, after all the times we bled as a team?"

The Spearmaker's voice was even keeled. He stood up slowly next to Bret.

"Let this go, Bron. There are no sides here—we are the People. The last thing we need now is this false, divisive poison spreading. This is madness and beneath you, Bron. This is a threat to the People. I will end it if need be. You have my word."

Chief Sev blasted the entire Gher.

"AASH, SHUT UP! There will be no more talk of this! There will be no fighting. I'll banish anyone who disobeys. Bron, it was Zig's fault, not Bret's. Take the pain. Get over it. Stop this chaos—we have to figure out a way to feed the People. Winter is coming."

The hunting teams left to do their duty. Bret turned to Aash and placed a hand on his shoulder.

"Thank you, brother," the little hunter said. The Spearmaker nodded warmly in response. The little hunter left to hunt as well. Chief Sev and the Spearmaker were the only ones remaining in the Gher.

"Aash, what has gotten into you? I was counting on you, the son of The Eagle Feather, to be the voice of reason, to help me nip this idiocy in the bud before it gets out of hand," Chief Sev admonished.

"Yes sir," replied the Spearmaker. "I tried that, Bron wasn't buying it. Then I gave it to him straight, in terms they'd all understand. The People come first."

"Agreed," the Chief eventually said, then he changed topics. "Do you think we should reorganize the teams, and if so, how?" This discussion lasted into midday and the Spearmaker returned to his cache of broken spears.

Emil finished his chores in the scalding sun and brought his father a water pouch. Papa thanked Babo and scratched the back of Cloud's ear. The fiery heat was shimmering up in hazy waves off the grassy plain.

Papa peered at the glossy horizon for a long moment, then studied his son and the white wolf. Aash brushed his hand over Emil's forehead. "Drink more water, Babo—the sun is angry today," Papa said.

Emil brought Papa another glistening fresh water pouch. The boy drank deeply and ran off with his white wolf. He sipped water while watching his son and Cloud play fetch with a stick. The white wolf obeyed Emil's every command. Papa imagined a pack of the People's wolves corralling a herd of bison toward the cliff.

Emil's right. I've seen wolves panic prey into ambush. A wolf pack is the ultimate hunting team. There is something to this, Papa thought. Can we train Cloud to do this for us? If we use fire, wolves, and brave hunters, why not? We need more wolf cubs...

Five good men.

Gone with the wind.

There has to be a better way.

Chapter Four
Jungle Lore

"He who doesn't go to war roars like lions."
-Rajput Proverb

BANKS OF SILVERY MORNING mist floated up through the forest as the false dawn gave way to the true. The melodious songs of the night loons yielded to the cheerful chirping of the day birds. There had been no sign of the Sabretooth in six moon cycles.

Papa felt the first twinge of chill in the air. He hoisted his ash spear and motioned for Emil to quietly follow into the woods. Emil and Cloud followed Papa until they were deep in dark canopy. The sky was barely visible and they could only hear the birds chirping from the branches above. Papa sat still, holding Cloud and made the silence sign. After a while, the bird chirping died down and then stopped. Cloud sniffed something and went off stalking down the hill. The birds began chirping again at this movement.

Papa asked his boy:

"Did you see how the birds started chirping when Cloud moved? As quiet as a wolf glides, the birds see all. Use the birds. They will tell you if you are stalking or being stalked. Babo, the ability to stay perfectly still is the most important skill in the forest. Even if the wind is against you, even if you are seen, you have a chance if the animal or enemy is confused."

Emil observed, "So, Papa, we should first stop still in thick forest until the birds go quiet. Then, if we hear the birds again, some animal or person is moving close."

Papa smiled. "Good."

Papa pointed to a bush on the far side of the valley and asked Emil what he saw. Emil noticed, "A bunch of little birds are flying up out of the bush."

Papa asked, "Why are they doing that, Emil? Which way are they flying?"

Emil thought about it and offered, "Something spooked them, there must be another animal very close to that bush now. They flew away west. It's coming from the east."

"Exactly, Babo," replied Papa, "this is how to think. Now why does Cloud hunt so well?"

"He can run really fast, Papa, and has sharp teeth, and can smell things very far away," said Emil.

"Exactly," said Papa. "Predators and prey animals have better senses of smell than us, but the wind is also our friend. Now let's imagine you are a tiger or a bear." Emil gave his best growl.

Papa grinned. "So, if a bear wanted to hunt something in that bush, how should it stalk?"

"Upwind," noted Emil. "I mean it should stalk, so the wind is blowing in its face."

They watched Cloud emerge into a clearing below upwind, silently stalking into heavy bushes. Emil noticed, "Papa, Cloud is hunting into the wind just like you said!"

"Good," observed Papa, "Now let's say you are hunting something dangerous, a tiger, alone. Where is the most danger?"

"Everywhere!" Emil exclaimed.

Papa snorted darkly.

"Yes, Babo, only fools hunt tigers alone. Imagine the hunt from the cat's point of view. Prey animals have a great sense of smell. It will always try to approach into the wind. When stalking alone, it's impossible for one person to track and watch all four directions. You don't have to. The predator danger is from two areas that you aren't watching, downwind and behind you. Imagine the wind is blowing from your left to right. As you track you can see in front of you. The greatest danger is to your right or behind you. The wind shows you the danger direction. You know where it will likely come from."

Emil recounted: "First we go quiet and listen for the birds, then if it's an animal we know how it uses the wind. Papa, you are so smart!"

Aash laughed and admitted, "No, little one, I didn't think of all this. Your opa taught me this, just as I am teaching you. Do you remember his name?"

Papa knelt down so they were eye to eye.

"His name was Kishor, little one, and the most important thing he taught me is real men are strong and gentle, Emil. Always remember this, my son. A real man is strong because life is hard. He supports his family and friends and fights fiercely for them when needed. However, mostly he's gentle. He is kind and respectful to others. I've learned the best warriors aren't the biggest, strongest, or loudest, but men like this. There is nothing deadlier than a good man fighting for his family or friends. You need both strength and compassion, Emil. This balance is vital in life. One is useless without the other. Always remember this."

"Strong and gentle," Emil repeated. "Strong and gentle."

"Emil, it isn't easy to live this way. We must constantly work at both," Papa recalled.

Papa cupped his hand under Emil's chin. "I see all of this in you already, Emil. You will be a better man than your papa in every way. Be smarter, stronger, and kinder. You must work at this constantly and never, never, never quit."

A nearby bush parted as Cloud returned with a small water bird in his mouth. He dropped it at Emil's feet with a toothy grin. Emil scratched the back of Cloud's head behind the ears and hugged the young white wolf's shaggy neck. Papa picked up the water bird and inspected it. Cloud had stalked and killed it cleanly, but brought it back untouched for Emil. Papa watched the two of them, slowly shaking his head in amazement.

One bright sunny morning, Emil and Papa went out looking for flint stones. Cloud stayed with Mama and the boys hunting eggs. Before leaving, Emil took Cloud's head in his arms, ordering, "Guard Mama and the boys." Cloud licked Emil's face and obeyed. Mama and Papa both beamed, watching their little son and his white wolf.

The sun was now a heavy orange fireball high in the late summer sky. Papa led the way into the wooded thicket as shimmering waves of fiery heat reflected off the parched brown grass. They squinted up to see birds circling over the next small hill. A massive hairy boar carcass lay on the ground ahead. A glossy black raven cawed loudly in a nearby apple tree. Papa had an uncomfortable thought. He quickly helped Emil climb the nearest tree. He said, "Wolves are coming, little one—be still and learn their wisdom." Emil was confused.

A large pack of wolves treaded cautiously out of the forest, into the clearing. They sniffed the wind then began savagely devouring the carcass. As the pack left, the raven came down from the tree and finished off the greasy scraps.

"Papa, did the raven tell the wolves about the boar?" asked Emil.

Papa nodded. "Yes, Babo, wolves and ravens have a pact. The ravens from up high can see almost everything. The wolves have the sharp teeth needed to break tough animal hides. They help each other. This way both eat together what they couldn't see or eat alone."

Emil and Papa often spent time quietly observing wildlife from trees. Emil learned the language of the forest. All forest creatures have several distinct calls depending on the situation. The People could identify and imitate them all, and in time so could Emil.

Emil came to grasp the incredible value of just sitting perfectly still, listening intently, and quietly watching the environment around you. He learned which plants and fruit were good to eat, and which were poisonous. The boy absorbed which plants to squeeze over an open wound, and the ones to chew if you had a bellyache.

Emil was learning fast. They'd occasionally spend moonlit nights in a tall tree. Papa taught Emil many predators are nocturnal, especially the big cats. One clear, starry night they were in a tree by the river. The toads were croaking as the crickets chirped up a storm. They heard the shrill screech of an alarmed monkey. Emil whispered, "Papa, that is a monkey warning call. He must be in a tree by the water. He's seen a panther or a tiger stalking close."

The night suddenly came alive in a concert of sounds. Hearing the monkey, a spotted deer whistled its warning call, "Phreww, Phreww!" The fear spread to a peacock who let out a disturbed call of "Miaooo, Miaooo!" The whole forest was alarmed and alert. The toads near the bank stopped croaking; even the crickets were now silent. Every animal in the jungle knew the same thing. Beware, a stalking tiger is near!

Emil heard fierce growling echo melodiously through the trees. Then followed shrieks of scattering monkeys. An agonized, abrupt wail shot through the darkness. Emil gave Papa a befuddled look. All the animals had plenty of warning to escape the big cat.

Papa whispered, "Tigers do this to monkeys. The monkeys see the cat and are perfectly safe up in a big tree. The cat roars fiercely and scrapes the tree. The terrorized monkeys think it can reach them. Some panic and jump to switch trees, and the tiger usually catches one."

The forest sounds had told them this story. It was as if they'd seen it in broad daylight instead of hearing it by moonlight. Emil knew a stalking tiger had been spotted by the monkeys. This was between his tree and the river. The cat passed by north of Emil's tree at some distance. It then spooked the deer and peacocks. Then it circled back to the riverbank before returning to the monkey trees. The wind even told him the tiger had stalked the monkey tree from the east. Emil pointed to his palm to indicate their location. He traced a finger around it to show the beat the tiger had stalked. Papa checked the wind. He put a proud hand on Emil's shoulder, smiling in the darkness.

"Competence makes bravery easier, Emil. Put the time in. The People respect this. Finally, when things get crazy, make sure you don't. Knowledge can help with this."

The graying light of a fresh day gradually filtered into focus. Emil and Papa climbed down the tree at dawn. Papa showed Emil they didn't need the river for water. Papa found some stumpy grass stalks and tied it around both their ankles. They walked home through the damp early morning forest. The grass collected the morning dew from shrubs and bushes. They were able to drink by wringing the grass stalks over their mouths. Emil thought this was a great trick.

They made it back to the village just as it started to rain that morning, Papa left to fix a knife while Emil cuddled with Cloud in the Gher and told Mama about their night. Mama watched as Emil taught Cloud to stay still or be quiet on command. Then the wolf took a rainy nap.

Mama asked, "Emil, do you know why the people consider wolves to be the wisest animals?"

She took Emil in her lap. "Wolves are fierce hunters—as a team they can hunt anything. A pack is a family. They are tender and play together. Lions or bears will kill strange cubs. Wolves never do this. The pack adopts them. The old wolves teach the pack what they have learned, and are taken care of by the pack just like the cubs."

Mama went on, "Wolves, just like people, need each other. A lone wolf is very rare and rarely lasts into the tough winter. They know winter survival requires hunting big animals. They can only do this as a team."

Mama offered, "I can show you a game that hunters like your opa played, called Eagle Eye?"

Emil was excited to play and Mama explained the rules. First, she would pick ten to fifteen items and put them on a hide. Emil was allowed to look at them closely. She then covered them all with another hide. He had to name all of the items. Emil could only remember five items the first game. He whined, "Mama, this is too hard."

Mama told Emil to reset the game and cover the hide. Lulu named all of the items. Emil was impressed. He knew it would take a lot of practice to play this game as well as Mama.

The best part of the day was the evening fires after all the work was done. Emil was cuddled up with Cloud and asked, "Is a raven the smartest animal?" All of the nearby children inched closer, hoping Lulu would tell one of her famous stories, or teach them a new song.

Mama took a sip of water and began a favorite story.

"There was once a little raven family that lived in a tree. A big old black python lived in a hole nearby. Every time the ravens had new eggs, the snake would climb up and eat them. The ravens couldn't fight the snake. They asked their friend the monkey for help. The monkey told the Papa raven to fly to the nearest man village and fly off with a flint pouch. 'Let the men chase you, drop the pouch on the snake's hole,' the monkey said. The Papa raven did just this. The men angrily chased him to the hole. The big old python came out hissing and confused by all the noise. The startled men killed the snake. Now the raven eggs would be safe."

The children cheered. Everyone knew monkeys were wise creatures.

"Who was stronger, the big snake or the little monkey? Who won here?" asked Papa.

Emil replied, "The big snake was stronger, but the monkey was smarter, Papa, so he won!"

Papa added, "Always remember this, Babo, always."

Emil stated, "I hate snakes, they are bad, they killed Dori."

Mama added, "No, Emil, snakes aren't evil, they are animals trying to survive. They can be very dangerous, so we avoid them and kill them if we must."

Papa agreed, "Mama is right, Babo, they aren't bad creatures. The way they slither, and their venom just seems more sinister than a lion's claws, or a bear's paws."

Emil giggled. "It rhymes!"

"Lion's claws
Bear's Paws
Snake's jaws
Are we scared?
Naw, Naw, Naw!"

It was a silly little ditty. Somehow, it just caught on. With the kids at first and then Bret. The little hunter added it to his morning hunting ritual. He would belt out this silly rhyme while saluting the sun with outstretched arms. Then he'd take a big gulp of water and float into the woods like a silent wraith. Bret almost always made meat, and rarely had so much as a scratch when he returned. Everyone saw this.

Hunters are a superstitious lot. It seemed to work for Bret. *Why not try it?* They all needed a good-luck charm or talisman after the bison hunt. One morning Leif followed suit. His team brought a pair of elk that day, with no injury.

They all began singing the rhyme darkly before all hunts. Even Bron.

Chapter Five
The Running Boy

"Just because you see the lion's teeth, don't assume that the lion
is smiling."
-Al Mutanabbi

EMIL WAS HELPING PAPA make spears when the black
crows were still announcing morning. He was playing with a
flexible green stalk of wood when it snapped back. This sent
a round pebble flying across the village. Cloud immediately
raced off to retrieve the pebble for Emil. "Papa, why does it
fly so far?" Emil asked.

Papa was very surprised by how far the pebble had flown.
He had Emil do it again. The little boy surprised his distracted
father by cuddling him. He quickly licked the side of Papa's face,
giggling. "Wolf Kiss...! Wolf Kiss!" Papa chased him down to

tickle him in response. The wrestling match was on! Papa would teach him a new wrestling move each time.

Bret approached their Gher humming the silly ditty with a grin. "He wrestles better every time, Spearmaker. It won't be long before he thrashes you!" the little hunter observed.

Bret had broken his spear. Papa shook hands and returned with a limber light spear. Bret twirled the new spear, asking, "This is well made, but may I have a heavy thrusting spear?"

Papa hesitated. "Yes, Bret, of course. I thought the lighter spear would be better for the game only you can hunt. No one else of the People can run down a gazelle alone. What other hunter has caught enough fish to feed the whole village?"

Bret eyed Papa with a wry, knowing look, then smiled. "Yes, Spearmaker, I'll keep the light spear." As Bret left them, Papa motioned Emil close.

"Bret moves like a ghost through the forest. The heavy thrusting spear we use for mammoth or bear is hard for him to use. The others ignorantly tease him. Bret caught enough fish to feed us all, when the heavy rains kept other game away. The People forget."

Papa added:

"Babo, people only trust someone who tells the truth. Something I wish I'd also learned at your age is this. It's almost equally as important to tell the truth in the kindest way possible. Always try not to lie, though sometimes there are dark truths and white lies. A young hunter on my team died a horribly painful death, from a school of vipers, crossing a stream during the war. Our hunting team made a pact to tell his family he passed peacefully from a spider bite in his sleep. This is a white lie, but once you get this habit, lying is a slippery slope, Babo."

Emil observed, "So it's true Bret isn't strong enough for a big spear. It's also true he can do things with a light spear no one else can. No one likes to be teased. So, Papa, you told him the truth, but the nicer truth. I like Bret. He makes all the boys laugh, and he's so fast."

Then Emil declared, "Papa, I have to get my egg pouch so I won't be late!"

Aash smiled, watching Emil run off with Cloud at his heels. There was something to the way the green stalk of wood bent. It had some power within that Papa needed to understand.

The leaves had changed colors. The Autumn Feast was coming. There would be races and contests of strength.

Emil loved to run. He was fast but some of the older boys were faster. He would rarely win the first races. Mama noticed Emil would do better as they ran races. By race ten, Emil was always close to the front.

The boys headed back to the village during the hottest part of the day. Emil said, "Mama, If I could run like Cloud then I'd win the big race."

Mama suggested, "You run fast, Babo. If you really want to do better, practice running extra between now and the Feast."

Emil declared, "But Mama, no boy is as fast as Mats, and Kilan runs so fast too."

Mama replied, "Yes, those boys are very fast. All people have natural gifts. In a few things like sprinting you are just born fast. Assuming they both practice hard, a naturally slow runner can get much better, but he'll never beat the dedicated natural sprinter. In most things, however, hard work and practice make all the difference. Anyone can get better at anything if they believe in themselves and put in the hard work and practice.

"Emil, do you know how important running is to the People? Not even Bret, our fastest runner, can hope to catch a gazelle in a sprint. Our hunters will chase them half the day until they can't run anymore. We hunt as much with our legs as our spears."

"Wolves like Cloud hunt that way too!" Emil exclaimed. Mama smiled that he remembered.

Back at the village, Papa was carving a notch into the end of the green wood stalk when he saw them. He jumped up to give them both a hug and a kiss.

"Papa, Papa, I ran fast today. Mama said practice and I might win the Feast race!" Emil said.

Papa suggested, "You'll certainly get better with practice. I want to win the spear throw contest. We can practice together."

Emil watched Papa balance a heavy hunting spear onto the notch of the green wood stalk. "It's too big, Papa," observed Emil.

Papa looked at it again. His boy was right.

The next day Emil and Papa started practicing running and throwing together. Emil was too small for a heavy hunting spear. Papa carved him a very small practice spear and taught him the right throwing technique. Throwing was a key skill for the people. All the children practiced with rocks daily.

Throwing was very hard for Emil the first day and Papa was also a bit out of practice. Emil could not throw very straight or far. His arm got very sore. The boy threw the spear down in frustration, yelling, "I can't do this!"

Papa commanded, "Emil, pick that up!" in a stern voice. Then he made Emil throw ten more times. The results were the same. Then Papa started laughing.

Emil started to tear up. "Papa, you are laughing at me."

Papa scooped Emil up, "No, Babo, never. I'm thinking if we were hunting together today, some lucky deer or bison would get to live another day! It's only your first day throwing. I have no such excuse," and he laughed some more, until Emil started laughing too.

Papa put Emil down, kneeling until they were eye to eye. "Listen, Babo: whenever something is bad or tough, let's figure out a way to laugh at it, and then don't quit."

Then he asked Emil, "Do you know how many seasons I've practiced throwing? This is just your first day. Practice hard and someday, Emil, you will be the best spearman of the People.'

Cloud had retrieved Emil's last throw and dropped the small spear at Emil's feet. As it glistened in the green grass, Papa had an idea.

"Let's head back, Babo," he said.

The next day Mama and Emil returned early with eggs and berries. Papa was sitting with a scowl on his face and a cut on his forearm. There was a shattered spear shaft at his feet. He was wrapping an herb poultice on the cut. Mama checked the cut and expertly rewrapped the poultice around Papa's arm.

Papa shrugged.

"Thank you. It's just a scratch. That shaft was too light for a heavy spear but not flexible enough for a light spear. I knew better. I thought I'd still pound a spear out of it. Then this happened. Learn from my mistake, Emil. We all make mistakes. It's usually not the first mistake that gets you into big trouble, but the second one. In this case, my first mistake was trying to force this weak shaft into a spear when I knew better. The second mistake would be to ignore this dirty little scratch. The poultice for cuts is needed to avoid sickness in this heat. Avoid the second mistake, Babo."

Papa motioned them closer to show them something. He'd carved a narrow groove into the notched green wood stalk. Emil's smaller spear was whittled down further to fit this groove. The little spear or dart was now a snug fit to the new throwing stick.

Papa took the loaded throwing stick and pointed at a mounted hide target. It was over twice as far as a man could throw a heavy spear. "Watch this," he announced.

Papa took a big step and threw it over his head at the target with a powerful snapping motion. He remained holding the green throwing stick, but the slim dart had hummed out of his hand with great power. It struck the target with great force, nearly shattering it.

Emil and Mama beamed. Papa remarked, "This will help the People hunt and defend ourselves. We can each carry six of these smaller darts. It's more than double spear range."

Mama responded, "I have an idea too," and headed back to the Gher.

Papa told Emil, "Babo, let's wait and practice a bit more before we tell everyone, OK?"

"Why, Papa?" asked Emil curiously.

Papa replied, "Often with new things or ideas, Babo, it is better to show people than tell them."

Emil helped Papa carve more smaller throwing darts. It was soon time for the daily tasks.

As they passed the Gher they heard singing inside.

"Mama," said Emil with a big smile.

Papa looked at Emil and remembered when Emil was a baby. Lulu would sing him to sleep with a sweet lullaby. It always brought peace to his heart. Aash thought there was something truly sacred in a mother's love. Emil loved singing too. It wasn't something Papa was good at or did often anymore. He liked hearing Mama and Emil sing together. Emil had Lulu's rosy spirit. Papa hoped this trait always stayed within Emil.

He picked Emil up and gave him a big kiss. Most men in the village were more reserved with their affection. Papa knew this was silly. Nothing is guaranteed in life. Besides, he thought, *someday soon this little cuddle monkey will be a strapping young man. A powerful hunter is likely too embarrassed to be kissed by his little old papa.*

Back in their Gher that night Mama had a gift for Papa. She had stitched together a beaded deer hide quiver with a strap. It held six of the new spear darts and could be worn on Papa's back.

Papa examined the new quiver with great care. Mama had put a great deal of thought into the design. It was lightweight but tough. The flap fit in a way that was secure and allowed for running. He gave her a big hug of thanks and quipped, "If only I was still hunting."

She replied, "I know you miss it. It's also good to have you close during the day, and Emil has never been happier."

After their daily tasks were finished, Papa and Emil consistently practiced for the Autumn Feast. Papa was having a tough practice session. Today he just wasn't hitting the target.

Emil was giggling darkly. "Papa, well at least we won't have to build a new target today!" he voiced with a mischievous grin. Then he ducked as Papa tried to grab and tickle him.

Papa smiled, thinking, *Babo's listening and learning.* Then he closed his eyes and took in four deep breaths. In his mind's eye he saw himself focused on the target. He opened his eyes, took a step toward the target and threw with a long smooth motion. The spear dart shattered the target.

Emil was running much faster than before and his throwing improved. On one throw Emil had great focus and hit the target dead center. He yelled, "I did it! Papa, I did it!" while Papa scooped him up.

Papa told Emil:

"You did it once, Emil, you can do it again. If you practice enough you will be able to hit the target every time. This is true of most things, Emil. Do you remember the first day you threw? Do you remember how hard it was? We didn't quit. We never, never quit, and now today you hit the target like a real hunter. This is called grit."

Emil beamed. "Papa, do you really think I can be on a hunting team like you?'

Papa announced, "Yes, if you keep running and practicing. You already know how to use the wind and listen to nature. Tracking and hunting are very important skills for a hunter. You actually already do the most important thing."

"I do? What's more important for hunting than running and throwing, Papa?" Emil asked.

Papa suggested:

"Babo, thinking and using your imagination is the most important thing about doing anything. We are not the strongest or fastest animals, Emil. Our minds allow us to survive because we can think. The leader of a hunting team must be able to throw and run well. He doesn't have to be the best, though. He must, however, know how to imagine, stay calm, and think."

"How do you practice being calm, Papa?" Emil asked.

"That's a great question, Babo," replied Papa.

Emil watched his papa take four very deep breaths with his mouth, holding each breath for a count of four, and then exhaling for a count of four. Then Papa began breathing deeply through his nose. Inhale hold, exhale hold, then repeat, with each motion to a count of four.

After a few minutes, Emil tried this way of breathing and felt very calm, quiet, and focused. "I feel very calm, Papa!" he proclaimed.

"Everyone is different," Papa stated. "I do this type of breathing before hunts, fighting, or anything important. I even do it at dances."

"Why dances, Papa?" Emil asked.

"I also did this the first time I danced with your mother," slyly admitted Papa.

"Why, Papa?" asked Emil. "Mama is so nice."

"You will see someday, little one," smiled Papa nostalgically, "now let's go, hunting lesson!"

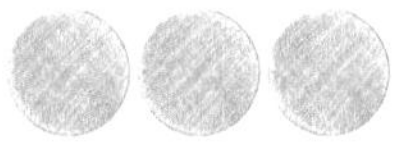

They made their way into the forest with the white wolf. Emil was singing a new rhyming song he'd just made up, just like he always did.

"Bears eat Pears
Parrots eat Carrots
Ferrets eat Parrots
So, Ferrets eat Carrots!"

Emil giggled with glee. Papa munched a pear, wondering if ferrets in fact actually ate carrots. Aash knew Bret would adopt the song. The Spearmaker pondered if the hunters would pick up on this new tune as well. They had begun sarcastically singing these child songs while leaving to hunt. You couldn't argue with the results. They were making meat with no team injuries in many moons. It was fast becoming habit.

Papa could just picture the hilarity of Leif's fierce hunting team actually singing this silly little ditty every morning.

Life would be a lot easier for the People if bears only ate pears, thought Papa. A grizzly was so fierce, many of the People would never mention it by name. Instead, they called them, "The Brown Ones."

Chapter Six
The Autumn Feast

"A lion can run faster than we can, but we can run farther."
-Ethiopian Proverb

THIS WAS THE SPECIAL day of remembrance every fall. The People gave thanks for the blessings of life and honored their ancestors. The village came together to celebrate the Autumn Feast with the story of the beginning. There were contests of speed and strength.

The morning began with special sweets made of nuts, berries, and honey. The village Elder told the story of the beginning. A great flood had come over the world. A sturdy Auroch had sheltered the first People, giving them his meat for food, his hides for warmth, and the strength of his spirit forever.

Despite tales from the past, it was rare for the People to take large dangerous game such as mammoth or bear directly. The hunters were brave enough. More often than not gathering mattered more than making meat. The dilemma of hunting with heavy spears and clubs led to a dark joke. If you were close enough to introduce yourself to big game animal, it returned the favor tenfold. Hoofs, claws, tusks, or fangs at close range more than left a mark. The smaller game, like deer, rudely just ran too fast. "It must be our bad breath," was the old hunter's rueful lament.

Actually, hunting was mainly persistence, running the prey to exhaustion. All prey animals can outrun men in a sprint. However, only humans sweat, which means they can run all day in the hot sun. A hunter only has to keep a deer in sight and keep it running all day with no rest. Deer overheat and must slow down or stand still. At this point, sometimes the spear wasn't even necessary. The animal had actually been killed with legs and lungs. This is how important running was for the People.

Winter was thus a very dangerous season for the People. Gathering fruits and nuts was more challenging. It's also hard to run deer to exhaustion in heavy snow. Often, many of the People present at the Autumn Feast wouldn't survive the rigors of the coming winter. The merciless cold and lengthy periods with scant food took their toll. This was all about to change for the better, however.

The People wore colorful paint and festive feathers as Lulu led them in song. At twenty-one winters old, she was young to be the People's song leader. Her voice and song memory were unmatched. Lulu could name the People's ancestors back for many generations. Emil and Papa always loved listening to Mama sing.

However, it was her talking animal stories that all the children eagerly anticipated. Truth be told, more than a few of the adults did so as well.

Lulu gathered the excited children and honored this tradition with her usual jubilant smile.

"A long time ago a woodpecker, a turtle, and a deer were the best of friends. One day the deer got caught in a hunter's snare. He started crying because he knew the hunter was coming. His friends helped him. The woodpecker told the turtle to bite through the rope while he delayed the hunter. The woodpecker then dove on the hunter, pecking his head until he ran back into his Gher. The hunter came back wearing a thick fur hat. The turtle was a good friend, but slow like turtles are. He finally bit through the rope, freeing the deer when the hunter was almost there again. The deer ran off, but the hunter caught the turtle, saying, 'I'll eat this now,' and began carrying it home in a pouch. The friends stayed loyal. The deer told the woodpecker, 'When I lure the hunter away, free the turtle.'

"The hunter was almost back to his Gher again when he saw the deer lying lame on the ground. *Deer taste much better than turtle*, he thought, so he dropped the pouch to get the deer. The deer led him on a merry chase while the woodpecker freed the turtle. The deer knew he needed to distract the hunter for a long time because the turtle was slow, so he led the chase to a dark cave he knew had a hole in the back. The hunter thought he'd trapped the deer, who just ran out the back hole. It took a long time for the hunter to figure out he was alone in the cave, and by then all three of the animal friends were safe."

The children howled in delight. Lulu bowed, declaring, "All the friends were so different, but also similarly loyal and brave. This is the blessing of true friends."

Bret came over, greeting Emil and Papa warmly. He smiled at Emil, who was hopping up and down, while shaking his fingers and loosening his jaw. The little hunter went over to help Papa carry the heavy wooden throwing targets.

Kilan came over to Emil, watching his warmup. The bigger boy said, "That silly monkey dance won't help you in the race, Emil. You're the turtle and I'm the deer, just like in the story."

Emil stomped his feet, losing his temper. "Kilan, your face is proof the Sky Spirits like to laugh!"

Bret was back and had witnessed this exchange. The little hunter motioned Emil over to him.

"Young buck, you're all tense again now. Loosen up, c'mon, it's almost race time! That boy was just trying to get in your head. You thumped him a bit too harshly. That's fine. If a man talks the talk, he'd best walk the walk. Some men just need to chirp, let them. Now if it's bullying, I agree use your sharp wits rather than fists. Bullies won't stop until you do. But this wasn't bullying. My question is this: win or lose, why give that little dingleberry the satisfaction?"

"I shouldn't have said something back?" Emil asked.

"No, that's not what I'm saying—he started it," replied the little hunter. "I'm saying when you angrily stomp around, it shows he's gotten to you. Win or lose, never give them the satisfaction."

It was race time! The People watched elated with excitement as the boys all lined up. The Auroch horn sounded the start. The race was eight full turns around the great field. Mats, the fastest boy, jumped out to a clear early lead followed by Kilan. Emil was in the middle of the pack for the first four rounds. He was in third place by the sixth turn. On the seventh turn Emil was side by side with Kilan for second place. Mats crossed the final turn and won. Emil surprised the whole village by beating Kilan for second place.

Mats was given the prize necklace with the hoof bones of a swift red deer. All the other boys were surprisingly ordered to run the entire course again.

The Chief explained, "Boys, we only reward first place. The second-place hunter doesn't catch the deer. The second-best warrior does not come home. Never forget this."

Emil finished first in this second race. Papa was silent, but a keen observer would have caught the slight glint of pride in his eyes.

A few hours before dusk, it was time for the heavy spear contest. Each hunter got one throw. The targets were moved further back with each hit. Once again, no points for second place. Papa made it to the final three, but just missed with his final throw. Leif was awarded the horns of an Auroch as his prize. Sev gathered the hunters, saying the Spearmaker wished to speak.

Papa stood in front of the People and loaded the throwing stick. The hunters began laughing and teasing good-naturedly, asking if this was Emil's little spear by mistake.

Leif joked, "Aash, now that you no longer hunt, can you no longer lift a hunting spear?"

Bron cracked, "Look at that cute little spear! Aash, when you are killed by a charging mammoth, can I give it to my daughter?"

Dark laugher and muffled snorts rippled through the ranks of the People's hunters.

Papa calmly walked to the spot where Leif had made the winning spear throw. He said quietly, "Leif is our champion spearman," then walked backwards three times the distance from this spot. He smoothly checked the throwing stick and rapidly fired the six darts from his quiver in smooth succession. Papa got four clean hits and completely shattered two of the targets.

The hunters were not laughing anymore. Leif and the Chief sprinted to one of the shattered targets. *This was new power.*

The force of the darts was shocking. Every man present instantly grasped the potential benefits of the throwing stick.

Papa walked over, explaining, "We can stand off much safer away from big game, and rain down these darts on them from a distance. We use the heavy spear or club to finish if needed." Then he smiled. *Even down five hunters, we should survive winter with these darts!*

The Chief grasped this immediately and bellowed out:

"Each hunter must have these darts and quivers as soon as possible! Spearmaker, you will begin training the men with this weapon immediately. With these darts we can fight at greater range, as if we had three times as many hunters. Raindrops hit everything. If we all throw these darts together, so will we!"

Papa nodded. "This will help the People." *Winter is coming.*

This is how a curious little boy, along with some imagination, helped the People discover a powerful new survival tool.

Chapter Seven
Bears and Men

"Fear an ignorant man more than a lion."
-Kurdish proverb

THE FALL RAINS CAME with a thunderous clatter. Eleven full moons had passed since the last Autumn Feast. It would soon be time for the boys of eight winters to choose a mentor. Each mentor was responsible for training his charge. The Trials of Manhood came at twelve winters.

Hunting was difficult during the heavy autumn rains. The People turned to the great fish migration for food. Every season when the leaves turned bright beautiful reds, oranges, and yellows, vast schools of fish would return to the rivers from the Great Salty Waters. The entire village would pitch in to catch as many of the silvery pink-speckled fish as possible. Emil declared, "I want to catch the most fish!"

Papa replied, "Bret is the best spear fisherman in the village. It's harder than it looks because the fish are fast. It's hard to judge exactly where the fish is underwater."

"Will we see bears, Papa?" asked Emil.

Eagles and bears also preyed upon this vast fish bounty.

"Maybe," answered Papa, "but usually not if we are in a big group. It can be dangerous to go fishing at the Bear River alone during this time. The bears have to eat enough fish for their winter sleep. Did you know your mama has a great bear story from when she was a little one?"

"The bear that killed Cloud's pack was really scary," Emil mentioned.

Emil gave Mama the *oh, you have got to tell me this story look!* Lulu recalled the tale with her usual mirth.

"Well, it was also during the great fish run. I was a few winters older than you. Your oma and I were helping carry baskets of fish back to the village. We stepped through some brown berry bushes by the stream. We walked right upon a big mama bear and her cub. Oma dropped her fish basket, drew her knife, and slowly stepped in front of me. The mama bear barked loudly, swatted her cub to the side and stood up on her hind legs. There was a long quiet moment where both Mamas looked into the other's eyes, and at me and the bear cub. That mama bear standing up seemed big enough to blot out the sun. Then she roared so loud I thought it would shake every leaf from every tree in the woods. Oma screamed the battle cry of the People right back at her. Then it was quiet again. Mama put one hand on my shoulder, and we took a very quiet, slow step back. The mama bear did nothing. Oma and I took two more big, slow steps back, and the mama bear came back to the ground. Then her cub ran off behind her into the bushes. The mama bear gave us another long look, then ambled off into the bushes behind her cub. Oma and I walked backwards many steps and then got out of there quickly."

"Wow," Emil declared, "it was a good mama bear!"

Lulu smiled. "Yes she was. Oma would have fought her, but the bear could easily have killed us both. Later after we stopped shaking Oma insisted, as crazy as it sounds, she knew we'd be fine. Both Mamas locked eyes in fear, and knew each would fight for her cub. Each of them understood this, and both decided this didn't have to happen."

Papa grinned. "I dunno, I think I'd rather fight a Grizzly than take on Oma." Lulu slugged him in the arm, and they all had a good laugh.

The next day a village fishing party was carrying home full baskets. A shrill cry pierced from above. A pair of eagles were fighting over a silver fish high in the sky. Something was floating down lazily through the sky. Papa's sharp eyes spotted a glimmer of white in the meadow ahead.

"Eagle feather," observed Papa with a nostalgic smile.

Mama added, "Your eyes are so much better than mine."

"This explains much, dear wife," grinned Papa.

Emil ran off and retrieved the eagle feather. It was perfectly formed and a brilliant white. As he ran back to the group, it seemed they were all staring at him and whispering something.

Papa gave Emil a long look, and turned his head sideways with a quiet smile. Emil thought he saw moisture in Papa's eyes. Mama gently took Papa's hand. Aash looked at the white feather closely and ran his fingers through Emil's hair, giving his son a kiss on the forehead. Then Papa grabbed a basket and commanded, "Let's go or we will be late." He began briskly walking toward the river.

Emil looked at Mama. "Is Papa sad, Mama?"

"No, Babo, he's fine. Your opa used to wear a white eagle feather. You look so much like him sometimes, Babo. He passed only one winter before you were born. We all wished he had a chance to meet you."

"Papa says he was the best man he ever knew," recalled Emil. "But if I look like Opa Kishor, and Papa loved him, why did Papa look a little sad?"

"He was a great leader, but I remember how kind and tender he was to all of us in the village. You will understand someday, Babo," explained Mama. They caught up with Papa.

Back at the village that night, Emil crawled into Papa's lap and showed him a headband Mama had made so he could wear the eagle feather.

Papa cuddled his son and began with a smile.

"Do you know why your opa wore a white eagle feather? Think closely on this, Emil. A white eagle feather stands out anywhere in the green forest. It's so easily seen from far, far away by any man or animal. The man who wears a white eagle feather is supremely confident in his ability. He is telling this to every other man and animal in the world. I will give you this competitive advantage. Are you sure you too want to wear the eagle feather?"

Papa looked his son in the eye.

"I'll share what he taught me. I only concentrate on what I can control. This is me going out and believing in myself. This kind of man can do anything. The opposite is also true. Talk is cheap—first a man must believe in himself, even when the world doesn't, then he puts the work in. It's simple, but simple isn't easy. The People saw he wore the Eagle Feather, and it inspired them through rough days. They don't know your opa never wore it in the Gher with our family. He only wore this feather to fire up the hearts of our people and plant a seed of doubt in the Mountain Men. A good leader serves his people."

Papa choked up a bit. "When I think of my father, it's not the warrior I remember. When I was little like you, we found an injured baby mongoose after a flood. We tried to save it, but it was too far gone. I remember him holding it in his hand all night as it died. He said he didn't want it to die alone. This is who your Opa Kishor really was."

Emil hugged his papa and ran his fingers through the white eagle feather. *Someday, not now.*

The next morning Emil and the boys were helping carry fish from the river. Bret had filled four baskets of fish. Most of the boys snickered at little Bret behind his back, just as their fathers did.

Emil asked, "Bret, you never miss. How do you do that?" Emil kept asking fishing questions as they walked back.

Bret revealed, "There is no secret. The only thing I can control is believing in myself, then I practiced fishing, fishing, fishing."

This sounded very familiar to Emil.

Bret smiled. "Do you know who taught me this? Your opa, the Eagle Feather. They said I was too small to hunt. He argued I had great instincts and should be given a chance. I'll never forget him."

Emil saw slight motion off the trail. A red squirrel streaked down a tree after an acorn into a rocky patch of grass. There was a glint of reflection off the rocks as Emil ran over to investigate. He found a large, long, narrow piece of obsidian.

Bret looked at it and whistled. "Great find, Emil. This is perfectly shaped obsidian, you will have the best hunting knife in the village."

Emil handed it to Bret. "It's for you then—a great hunter should have it. You've taught me so much."

Bret shook his head. "No, Emil, you are too young to know its value. Warriors would fight over this. Thank you, but it's too valuable."

"You are my friend," replied Emil, and he placed the long black stone in Bret's hand. Emil ran off to rejoin the boys without a second thought. Bret was touched by this wonderful gift.

They caught up to the rest of the boys and the walking topic turned to fire making. Mats suggested using a firefly. Bret said nothing. Luca, one of the bigger boys, told Mats, "Everyone knows fireflies don't make fire," and all the boys laughed. Mats became quiet.

Bret motioned for Emil to pause.

"Did you see what just happened here? Most people resent if you correct them when they are wrong. It doesn't matter if you speak truth. Only correct people when it's important. Why correct Mats about fireflies and fire? Let him learn himself what everyone else already knows. Now if Mats was going to eat a poisonous fruit that he thought was safe, of course you tell him. Do you follow this?"

Emil shared this with Papa that night in the Gher. Papa agreed: "Bret is sharp, this is very good advice. It is another way of always asking ourselves the wise ancient question: is this virtue or vanity? He shared it only with you, because we treat him with respect. We can learn something from everyone, Babo."

"What does 'is this virtue or vanity' mean, Papa?" asked Emil.

"Virtue is simply doing the right thing; vanity is doing something so you feel good about it," replied Papa. "This is a simple but good test question our ancestors asked before making decisions. Think on this, my son."

Papa asked Emil, "Have you been training for the Autumn Feast—it's half a moon cycle away?"

"Yes," replied Emil, "I've been thinking about my mentor too. Papa, who would you choose?"

Papa liked to hear Emil was putting thought into this. The People in their wisdom had learned the value of a mentor, other than the father to train young hunters. This maintained fairness and allowed a father to just be a father.

"I can't answer that for you, Emil. You know it's a personal choice. The People have great hunters. If you do well in the games, you can choose anyone you want," replied Papa.

Emil tried the indirect route, "Of course, Papa, but if you were still a boy and choosing now, how would you do it?"

Papa responded only with a silent quizzical look.

Emil asked another question: "Papa, how did you choose the men on your hunting team?"

Papa grinned inwardly, appreciating his son's maneuvering. This was a fair question regardless.

"I chose my team based on two things. All of my men were very different, except they are all high character, and sharp."

Emil nodded, thinking deeply on all of this. There was only one choice.

CHAPTER EIGHT
THE DEER HUNTER

"Roaring lions kill no prey."
-Zulu Proverb

EARLY THE NEXT MORNING, well before sunrise, there was a quiet knock at the Gher pole. Bret was standing outside in full hunting gear. He told Papa, "Emil found this obsidian blade and gave it to me. He's very generous but too young to know its value. It's not right for me to keep it."

Papa examined it carefully, commented, "This is spectacular," then he handed it back to Bret. "Emil considers you his friend. This is his way."

Bret was taken aback by this generosity. "Amazing. Spearmaker, am I still the best tracker in the village?" Papa nodded.

Bret asked, "Then with your permission, allow me to teach my young friend Emil deer tracking. Chief Sev has given me a break from fishing and there is fresh deer spoor close to the village."

Papa called into the Gher, "Babo, this is your lucky day. No chores, instead the best deer hunter of the People will teach you how he tracks. Get your footpads, water pouch, some dried berries, and hunting kit."

Emil was so excited he was hopping up and down in the Gher getting ready. Emil had a good sharp knife and Papa had made him a small throwing stick with six darts.

Sunrise found Emil and Bret at the edge of a rocky, bushy meadow. It then opened up into thick wooded forest. Bret had them circle around this meadow to get into the forest.

They did so and entered the forest area. Bret paused and asked, "Emil, why didn't we walk straight through that low bushy area?" Emil shook his head.

"Snakes," explained Bret.

"It's late in the season and early in the morning. Bushy rock beds can have many dangerous forest vipers. Vipers aren't as common in the forest because the birds and squirrels they feed upon can avoid their reach up in the trees. In rocky country like this, with low bushes, the birds are closer to the ground. The bushes give great natural cover for hunting squirrels or rabbits. Brushy areas also provide the snakes with better cover from things that might eat them."

A lazy ray of sunlight gleamed down through the arboreal canopy. A speckled brown sparrow floated down into the edge of the rock bed after some worms. The bird hopped lower from branch to branch of a berry bush until it was almost on the ground. As if on cue, a hissing blur from under the bush struck the bird faster than any man could react. It disappeared back into the rocks. The sparrow wobbled shakily, and tried to spread its wings and fly. It just fell off the bush. Only then did the black-mouthed viper fully reveal itself with a spine-tingling hiss.

Bret motioned for Emil to step back further, saying, "Stay there but watch closely."

The little hunter reached his spearpoint close into the viper's area, holding the other end of the spear firmly with both hands.

"The People think vipers are fast. On the ground they're actually clumsy movers. They can't leap at you. They don't have to coil to strike, and their striking range is a bit less than their body length. Their speed, however, is all in the strike. This comes at lightning speed with great power."

Another grayish-brown blur struck the spear with a resounding crack. The force almost knocked it out of the man's hands. Bret chopped off the viper's head with the edge of the spear, and flicked the severed body back over his shoulder. The viper's headless body landed in a bunch of ferns. The separated head now lay in a small pool of fluorescent amber venom. Both head and body were each still striking out at any leaf they touched. Emil was shocked at this.

Bret walked back over to Emil and pointed down.

"Even hours after you kill it, a severed snake's head can still kill you. Never forget this. As you see, the headless body reflex is also to strike though it can't hurt you anymore. Snakes are most active when it's warm, but they never hibernate. A fire at night is very important to keep snakes away. They are attracted to one's body heat. Be very alert nights after rainy storms, when frogs are everywhere in the mud. The snakes are very active, gorging themselves. Now you know the dangers of vipers, and how to avoid them."

Now Emil was certain he hated snakes. "Snakes scare me," he admitted quietly to Bret.

"Me too," remarked Bret, with a wink, "but we are men, and men have to be brave."

"Why doesn't the venom kill you if you eat snakes?" asked Emil.

Bret replied, "I think the venom has to get into your blood. Are you ready to stalk deer now?"

Bret knelt and grabbed a small handful of dirt, tossing it in the air to gauge the wind. Then he took two small steps into the forest and stopped. He took a knee and whispered to Emil.

"First, always remember deer are one of the most dangerous animals in the forest."

Emil wasn't sure he heard the little hunter right. The boy listened closely.

He's focused and listening, thought Bret. Then he went on.

"Deer are fast and strong with sharp hooves and dangerous antlers. Bucks in fall mating season don't eat, they just want to fight anything they see. Lions and bears are stronger but much more predictable. Deer can smell so well and move silently. They appear right next to you before you know it. The wind flows higher up in the early morning, so they can't smell you as easily as the rest of the day. My trick is to make them think you are a deer too. Walk like them. Think of the air like a swirling river of water. You always want to circle downwind. If you can't do this ahead of you, back up until you can. Now watch my feet."

Bret was kneeling at the base of a small hill. He loaded his throwing stick with a dart and took two small steps, then one more step. He would start in a balanced slight crouch with his weight shifted on one foot. Then he would step forward with his other foot. He let his little toe touch down first before rolling down on the outside edge of his foot. The little hunter was using his feet like hands in the dark. If he felt something noisy underneath, he wouldn't step down. His head, however, was still up and his eyes stayed up on the horizon. Bret knelt down to one knee. He watched the ground for noisy twigs and scanned all the way around. The next thing Emil knew, he was already up the small hill. *Papa was right*, thought Emil, *he moves like smoke in the forest*. Bret motioned for Emil to try. The boy copied everything Bret did as he climbed up the hill.

"Not bad at all, little man!" Bret grinned. *The boy is a natural stalker, like his opa*, he thought.

"This is how a deer moves—learn this. First walk as slow as you can, and then slow down twice as much. If you step on something noisy, sit still for a while. Even if a deer sees you and runs off, you might still get it if you sit still. When you see a deer, it can be exciting. Do your papa's breathing exercise to calm down. Plan your approach carefully using as much cover as possible."

They stalked silently all morning until the sun was high in the sky. Bret did a deer mating call. Emil realized, *We are stalking into a potential bushy viper area*. He backed them up and around it. There was a slight movement to their side as Bret quickly fired a dart into a deer which seemed to appear from nowhere. The deer stumbled, thrashing loudly into the brush. Bret ran it down and finished it with his spear. Bret carved the steaming heart out and dabbed the boy's forehead and cheeks with warm deer's blood. Emil thought, *This is an honor. I have to eat some*. He took a big bite of the offered dear heart, even though it made him a little sick.

"It was your kill, not mine," offered Emil.

"No," replied Bret, "the stalking is the hard part. It was our kill. You moved well for your first hunt. We share this kill." *He's just like I was*, thought Bret.

Emil drank some water and ate a few berries as Bret quickly carved up the deer. He didn't want to linger in bear country and put the steaks in a large pouch. They worked back close to the village. There was another low, bushy field in front of them which Emil knew to avoid now.

As they walked Bret noticed Emil was unusually quiet for such a cheerful boy. He knew why.

"Emil, are you sad we killed the deer?" the little hunter asked.

Emil nodded. "I know we need meat. Stalking is fun, but I felt sad after we killed it."

Bret stopped and dropped down so he was eye level with Emil. "My friend, I feel the same way. Killing is a serious thing. When you kill something, you take away its life and its future. We only kill for food or defense. It's good you think of the animals. If it helps, remember it's a cycle. When we die, we turn into food for the grass which the deer eat.

"Is that older boy from the races still teasing you?" Bret asked.

"Kilan? No, he's a good friend now. Some of the other boys do sometimes, though. I don't give any dingleberries the satisfaction, just like you said," Emil replied. "Did you know Kilan has the smelliest farts in the village? Even worse than Bron. It's great, it always sends the girls running!"

Bret chuckled. "Now that's impressive. Though someday not long from now you may feel quite differently about the girls in the village, Emil. Our women and girls are as brave and harder working than the men. They admire strength, honesty, compassion and especially a sense of humor."

The little hunter reminded himself to watch his language around the boy, then told a snake story.

"A long time ago, the snake had bitten and killed many forest creatures. It started to feel really guilty. It asked the Sky Spirits to take away its venom. The Sky Spirits said, 'Doing this would leave you defenseless. We will change your nature so you rarely bite.' The other animals figured out the snake rarely bit anymore and became careless around it. The snake grew weak and listless. The Sky Spirits saw how bad the snake looked and asked, 'What's wrong now?' The snake replied, 'I feel better. I don't kill so much, but now all the animals step on me.' The Sky Spirits thundered, 'You foolish creature! We told you not to bite as much. Who told you to stop hissing?'"

This brought a smirk into Emil's eyes. "I can't wait to be a hunter like you or my papa."

Bret declared in a gentle voice:

"Good. Be more like your papa than me. The hunters tease him a bit about being the Spearmaker now. But they all know we need good spears or else. The Eagle Feather, your opa, was born a natural warrior, and such men are truly rare. He was both the most dangerous, and safest man I ever met. He was like no one else.

"Emil, your papa is different—he's as steady as they come. In a dangerous situation or real trouble, he's the first one you want by your side. The hunters would all choose your papa over any man currently in the village. We all have our talents. He's a rock for the People because he willed himself to be this way.

He's calm and determined. This is the kind of man you want to be."

Emil beamed at this and felt much better. He then naturally had a bunch more questions for Bret. "How many deer do we lose if we don't hit them right?" Emil asked.

"Too many. As you saw, they appear almost instantly. You can't always hit them well, some run off, and some are just country tough," Bret answered.

"Bret, what do you think would happen if a dart dipped in viper venom hit a deer? Could we still eat the meat?" queried Emil.

Bret thought then answered, "That is a very interesting question, Emil, very interesting."

They made it back to the village shortly before dusk. Emil ran up to hug Mama and excitedly told her about the great day, the deer, and the snakes. Mama held the hug for a long time and thought, *My little boy is growing up so fast.*

Papa thanked Bret for the day.

Bret replied, "This boy reminds me of the Eagle Feather. He asks great questions."

Papa forced a straight face. *This was the supreme compliment.* Bret shared Emil's question about using the viper venom for hunting. Both hunters agreed this was something to explore.

The People welcomed fresh venison after a steady diet of fish and fruit. Mama and Papa told Emil his deer was the best they had tasted. Emil's proud smile lit up his face at helping feed the People.

That night back in the Gher, Emil was still bouncing off the walls telling his parents all about vipers, deer, and how smart Bret was. Then just as quickly, he was sound asleep cuddled with Cloud in his sleeping furs.

This Autumn Feast was the most plentiful in memory. The throwing sticks and darts had greatly changed their lives for the better. Many of the young boys were now at the age of mentorship. Each boy must choose a mentor other than his father. Emil knew his choice and was nervous the hunter would be chosen before his turn.

The boy's up for mentorship drew marked bones out of a leather pouch to determine order.

Emil luckily drew the first bone.

Chief Sev congratulated him. "Which hunter will mentor you, Emil?"

Emil's giddy reply was, "Bret!"

This was greeted with hushed silence. This was not meant to be a slight, so much as surprise at the boy's choice. Leif was the strongest hunter in the village. Bron could wrestle two men at once. When the People looked at Bret, they saw a small hunter of only seventeen winters. He fished well, and could run fast, but wasn't even on a hunting team. The other two actually led hunting teams. The People were embarrassed for Emil's folly.

Bret was astounded by this honor of being chosen first among every hunter of the People. He'd never even been chosen before. The little hunter's eyes met Papa's with a silent promise. *Emil will learn everything I know about hunting and life. The stars have finally given me the chance to honor the Eagle Feather.*

In the very near future, the People would soon see the wisdom of Emil's choice. This day, however, aside from Emil, the only clear sign of approval was a fleeting spark in Papa's eyes. *Wise choice, Babo. They don't see what Bret is yet.*

Bret came over to Emil's family with his usual lopsided grin.

"Emil, Emil, Emil, I thought you were so much smarter than this. I'm truly honored. Tomorrow after daily tasks we will run, then track, then throw. Rest up, young buck."

Chapter Nine

Courage

"There lies a lion in every heart."
-Sikh Proverb

A CRISP BLACK WIND sailed ghoulish sounds through the moonlit clouds. The Sabretooth had killed in the valley. Its roar was an outrage at being hunted that carried the cat's fervent bloodlust to kill everything in the valley. Small furry animals shivered in their burrows, as the fearsome echoes haunted the hills.

Cloud woke up stiff legged and growling at this sound ringing in the distance. Emil hushed the white wolf. This telltale threat stabbed fresh nightmares of fear into the hearts of the People. A Sabretooth's roar carries over an incredible distance at night. Emil saw Papa was already armed and awake. He was looking in the direction of the Mountain River.

"The Sabretooth has just killed. It wants to kill all of us, Papa," Emil stated.

"Yes, Babo," uttered Papa, "but it's very far away tonight. Don't worry. We have a good fire and Cloud's nose. Try and sleep, little one."

Papa still threw another log on the fire and began sharpening his darts. He wondered, *Why would the big cat announce its presence with a roar?* Now they knew it was back.

At sunrise, Chief Sev sent a hunting team to the area the Sabretooth roars had come from. Bret, who usually preferred to hunt alone, joined the team. They returned shortly before dusk. Bret's typical lighthearted grin had hardened to stone. He reported to Chief Sev while handing him a small deerskin bundle. The Chief quickly called a council of warriors. Chief Sev opened the bundle to reveal an ivory-chipped axe blade made from the tusks of a mammoth. *Only the Mountain Men use this weapon.* There was finely dried blood near the base. *This was trouble.* The Chief let the weary hunting party eat before reporting. The hunting party wolfed down some fish and drank deeply from the water pouches offered to them. Bret finished first, and spoke for them.

"There's Sabretooth spoor all over the big hills by the Mountain River. It gets worse. We also found the partially eaten body of a Mountain Man. Also, fresh tracks from one of their hunting parties by the hill caves on our side of the river. They were moving fast and unbelievably trying to track at night. The great cat ambushed them on a narrow trail by the hill caves.”

“The Mountain Men cannot be allowed to hunt our lands, or others will as well. We must answer this aggression,” Chief Sev responded in a tone of worry.

Papa raised his hand to speak.

“We’ve not had war for many winters. The Mountain Men have better hunting lands than we do. It’d be truly foolish to risk war so close to the winter. Is it possible they were chasing the maneater, and it circled back to ambush them? Bret, how many came, did they hide their tracks?”

Bret replied, “It was a party of four. One was taken by the Sabretooth. At least one other was injured or limped. They hurried back across the river. Yes, they tried to hide their tracks.”

Chief Sev asked, “Spearmaker, are you saying the Sabretooth has killed so many Mountain Men they are this desperate?” Heads were shaking in disbelief. Night hunting carnivora was suicide.

Papa answered, “We haven’t heard this Sabretooth roar in eleven moon cycles because of Cloud. This morning the Mountain Men had already crossed back. They weren’t scouting to attack us. They hoped we wouldn’t notice. We should let this single intrusion pass.”

Bret raised his hand to speak. “One more thing—this Mountain Man hunting team tracked the Sabretooth across a river at night. This is incredible tracking skill, even if it is madness."

Chief Sev stroked his white beard quietly for some time. *A winter war would be deadly for the People.* "The Spearmaker is right. We let this pass for now."

After the others had left, Chief Sev motioned Aash over. They stepped out of earshot, away from the glow of the fires into the darkness. "Maybe your boy is right about talking to them," he said.

The Chief went on speaking in hushed tones.

"We just don't know and can't take the chance. The fish won't last and winter is coming. We don't have enough men to hunt and also guard the village against attack. They started the last war with a sneak attack. Then there is the maneater. We need a scout to sneak over and see if their village is preparing for war. It's very risky, but with luck, one good man could be back in a few nights with the answer. What are your thoughts, Spearmaker?"

Chief Sev lit his pipe. This illuminated Bret standing silently in the darkness right in front of them.

They both recoiled back in surprise, as the Chief's heart skipped a beat. Aash had reflexively drawn his knife at the shock. Despite being seasoned warriors, neither had in any way sensed the little hunter's silent approach. They both realized he'd been standing there the entire time. He could easily have killed them both.

"I'm the one," insisted Bret softly, stepping silently out of the darkness back into the firelight.

Bret let this fact sink in, then turned back to face them in a matter-of-fact voice.

"Emil is right. It'd be better to talk to them, but there isn't time. I'm fast, small, and quiet. That's what's needed to pull this off. They won't see me just like you didn't. I'll spend tomorrow night in a tree by the Mountain River and cross at first light. I'll watch their village and see if war is coming. I'll stay another night in a tree if needed, and be back the next day."

"If you are seen in their lands, that itself could start a war," warned the Chief.

Bret replied in the manner of someone who had thoroughly thought things through:

"Simple. I'll only carry weapons we've captured from other tribes. There are several hostile tribes to the north. I'll approach the Mountain Man village from that direction. If I'm spotted, I never come back. I'll lead their trackers due east, far away from the People. Send a hunting party to the hills by the river to watch for big smoke by the Mountain Man village. If you see smoke, it means I was spotted and they want war. I'll set a big fire and take a few of them with me. If they don't want war, but still spot me, I can lead them on a merry chase, but we all know their trackers are too good to lose in the end. It must be this way."

Chief Sev felt deep emotion and had to look away for a second. He realized how wrong he'd been, how wrong they had all been about this plucky little hunter. *A man cannot be judged by his appearance. The Eagle Feather was right to argue for him.* The little man was a natural warrior, swift of foot and mind, and devoted to the People.

Chief Sev said, "I'm going to find Leif. You two please meet me in front of my Gher."

The Chief had staked four burning torches in the dirt in front of his Gher. He greeted Leif and Bret. The Spearmaker showed up last with a bundle in his arms. Chief Sev began drawing in the illuminated dirt with a sharp stick. It was a rough map of the village, the Mountain River, and the terrain on the opposite side.

"I know their lands well from the war. We are here. The Mountain Man village is due east of us across the river. The river divides our lands flowing south to north. There are waterfalls to the north beyond the bend. The white water is too rough near the waterfalls. The terrain by the bend is rocky and full of caves. It's very hard to track there, and likely where the cat lives. The Sabretooth changes everything. We used to swim across at night well south of the falls. Then, instead of going straight for the village, we'd work our way north into the rocky country by the waterfall. At the waterfall we would head east. The rocky area gives way to deeply thick forest. There are two hills, a little one and a big one. Their village is between them to the south. The big hill is where you want to be. At the summit, you can safely observe their village. There is a great purple birch tree to watch from. Then get out quick. This is the path to take, but with the cat, now night movement is suicide."

Leif responded respectfully.

"I don't know how Bret gets across then. The Mountain Men watch the river for the Sabretooth from first light to dusk. It's too dark to try for the river tonight. We have to know fast if they are going to attack. The odd thing is the Sabretooth tracks. They just disappear by the river bend. I don't think the cat just swims over at night. Both us and the Mountain Men have traps set for him all along the shore south of the bend."

Chief Sev spoke next. "The Sabretooth must cross north of the bend somehow then."

"Nothing can cross safely in the white water," Leif said. "You either get sucked under or the falls get you."

Bret chimed in. "The good news is if the cat killed last night, he probably won't be hungry for at least a day or two. The bad is I'll have to cross by daylight, by the falls where they don't watch."

"Impossible," Leif said.

"No choice, brother," Bret said softly with his lopsided grin.

Leif, the big man, had to look away in awe. *This mission is pure suicide.*

The Spearmaker took a knee and unwrapped the bundle.

"We have this from the war. A pair of Mountain Man boots, some pouches, and an ivory axe. There are also two good knives. I also have a good light spear you might want."

The little hunter grinned.

"I've always wanted fur boots, though these are as big as a Gher. I'll take the water pouch and both knives. Leif, can even your strength lift that mammoth axe? Those men must be giants. This is a good little spear. Too good. They'd know it was one of ours. Spearmaker, can you make me a simple balanced shaft with a tempered wooden point? I'll leave at first light."

The Spearmaker turned his head warmly. "I'll fix these boots and have that sharpened stick for you at dawn."

Chief Sev ordered, "Bret eat as much meat as your belly can take tonight, then more. Get to sleep."

The next morning everyone in the village eyed Bret with a newfound respect. All knew full well the risks the little warrior was taking for the People. Papa had worked all night on the boots and the sharpened stake.

The little hunter wrapped the fur boots tightly around his ankles and twirled the new shaft.

"This is great, Spearmaker. I can run in them now. Careful, or I'll tell all the women you can make fur boots. The wooden stake is well balanced. Perfect. Thank you, Aash."

Bret handed Emil the obsidian stone—he hadn't finished carving a knife out of it. Emil gave Bret a hug. "No dingleberries, OK?"

"Smile, young buck, I'm a ghost in the wind. I want my black knife back tomorrow," Bret winked.

Chief Sev put an arm around the little hunter.

"The clouds show a decent chance of rain the next few days. This should help mask your movement. There are plenty of good caves by the big hill, but the cat could trap you in one. Whatever you do, avoid the big cave on the little hill. It's a deathtrap. Trust me on this, Bret.

"Listen to me, son. If it all goes bad, head southeast. East of the Mountain Village is another river, then nothing but open plains. You will never lose them there. To the southeast there are wooded hills, and eventually the snow mountains. I order you to return to the People from the south after a few seasons.

"There are hostile tribes all over. It won't be easy. I only know two men capable of doing this. You move as well as the Eagle Feather did. You can do this, Bret. I have all sorts of things for you to do when you get back."

Every hunter in the village clasped forearms warmly with Bret and wished him well. Then Bret was gone. He flowed swiftly and silently through fog and trees toward the Mountain River.

Chief Sev watched him go with mixed feelings. *I'm proud the People have a man as brave as you, little warrior. Forgive me for all the times we ignorantly teased you.*

Chapter Ten
Ghost

"The lion is valiant, the leopard treacherous."
-Afghan Proverb

THE LITTLE HUNTER MADE it to the waterfall when the young sun just peeked at the morning sky. A fine gray mist churned from the white water onto the hard, black granite. Bret was crawling low and slow with the spear shaft cradled in his arms. There was little chance anyone across the river could see him with the fog and spray. He kept an eye out for the cat, but knew the swirling river was the first danger. *Mighty Leif was right. The Mountain Men don't need to watch this area.*

He watched a log swirl at the water's edge down below. It was swirling and bobbing way too fast. The driftwood was down over the falls before it even made it halfway across the river.

Bret felt his body go cold. His skin seemed to contract tighter around him, making him feel smaller. He saw his pale reflection in a shallow rock puddle. The little hunter put his fear aside, and focused on what might happen to Emil and the little ones if war broke out. *You say you're a ghost in the wind, Bret. Prove it.*

He'd seen old tracks in the rocky woods coming and going before the granite. The last set of outbound Sabretooth tracks were headed northeast. Bret stayed this course right up to the edge of the overhang. *No harm will come to my People. Not on my watch.*

Think. Think. There has to be a way. The Sabretooth knows how. How does the cat do it? If the cat continued on this course it'd end up right at the bedrock overhang of the waterfall.

A fly seemed to buzz right out of the ground just over the edge in a spray of vapor. The little hunter blinked again. He panned behind him, then silently peeked down over the edge.

It's definitely flies, more than one.

It was a big scat. Herbivore scats are smaller and all things being relative, don't smell as bad.

At least a day old and from a well-fed carnivore. The Sabretooth has been down there over the edge, but why?

Bret took a deep breath. You can do it, man. You know how. He began to feel the determination wash over him. His face took a hard set. The little hunter's muscles tensed and his eyesight suddenly became very sharp. He slowly slid over the rocky edge. The little hunter landed gingerly right next to the putrid cat scat. Then it all made sense. *You sneaky Shaitan, grinned the little hunter.*

The impact and splash-back from the falls had eroded a partial cave-like rock path below and behind the waterfall. This is how the Sabretooth crossed back and forth unseen. Despite the watery smell, the scat next to him was still horrid. Bret thought, *I think I'll start eating more vegetables.*

He was certain the hidden rock shelter extended to the other side. There was a faint twinge of daylight down the tunnel. Nothing could be heard over the deafening roar of the falls. He forced himself to ignore the massive sheets of raging white water pummeling down with thunderous fury a few feet to his left. If the Sabretooth fits through, so will I. *If it's waiting in there, I'm already dead anyway. If I slip here, at least it'd be quick. Time to go.*

The little hunter stayed as far to the right on the slippery rock path as possible. He began crawling through the wet darkness, poking ahead with the shaft to probe for obstacles. There were none, and he was through to the other side rather easily. *This Sabretooth is something else*, he thought.

Bret cautiously peeked up over the smooth granite ledge on the far bank. Clear. The little hunter crawled slowly but smoothly across the granite to the base of the thick woodland. He crouched low, sitting perfectly still between a scraggly holly bush and a thick oak tree. He just listened and rested until the bird chirps returned. The little hunter took a swig from his water pouch, and reached for the crushed green camouflage paste. He applied a darker shade on his forehead and jaws, with lighter colors for his cheeks and under his eyes. Once he was sure he was alone, he quietly climbed the tree to get his bearings. The little hill was on the far side of a thick wooded valley. There was a game path and a dirty stream at the base of the valley about halfway to the little hill. Bret checked the sun and the wind. The clouds told him it would start raining soon. He checked his knives and settled down to wait for the raindrops.

It's a good rain. Hard enough to restrict visibility and muffle sound, but not too hard. Bret took advantage of this cover to stalk to the edge of the game path just before midday. The rainy fog gave way to a hesitant sunny rainbow. Bret was about to crawl across the muddy game path when he sensed it. Danger. The little hunter froze and held his breath at the base of a thick spruce tree. He was fully caked in mud and leaves. *It's great cover.*

There was slight movement downhill in his peripheral vision as a red deer silently sauntered out of the thicket to drink at the dirty stream. The deer cautiously tested the wind and began drinking. Out of nowhere, a long yellowish-brown log from the dirty stream struck the stag with a steaming splash. Powerful coils instantly wrapped around the stricken deer. Bret was horrified to realize the log was the biggest python he'd ever seen. The forest came alive with chirping birds and thrashing branches. Bret heard voices rapidly approaching. *Of course, it's a snake. A big snake. Always a snake*, he thought. *The Mountain Men were also stalking this deer.*

A red-haired giant stepped into the clearing right where the deer had emerged. *Is everything big here?* wondered Bret. *I'm in the land of monster snakes and ferocious giants*, thought the little hunter.

The python turned to face the man, as the rest of his hunting team came up to attack. Whirling ivory axes spun through the air, smashing into the great snake. The hissing python released the stag and shot straight for the big man with fangs glistening.

The red-haired giant deftly dodged the strike, and casually decapitated the great serpent with a single smooth axe stroke. Bret nodded silently at the giant's skill. The muddy streambank became a whirling circle of laughing Mountain Men trying to avoid each other, as well as the thrashing snake's body. The python's decapitated head was still biting when anything touched it.

Bret considered taking this opportunity to cross the game trail. He decided against it. *They're all stirred up and too close.* He was just uphill from them. The little hunter slid silently back until there was a fallen log between him and the trail. *I'll wait them out.*

Three burly Mountain Men hoisted the python's body over their shoulders, and made their way up the game trail. The redheaded giant followed with the stag slung over his shoulders.

Bret felt the wind change and avoided eye contact as they passed. The little hunter felt the bugs from a nearby anthill he'd missed on his skin. The knowledge he couldn't move to swat them off combined with the creepy feel of things crawling on him. The giant Mountain Man stopped, closed his eyes and sniffed the air. The fire ants were eating Bret alive. *Take the pain. Breathe. Breathe.*

Something bothered the giant, but he didn't know what it was. He put the stag down and looked around for a long moment, searching to his right with all his senses. The giant finally shook it off. *Maybe a hare or something. Certainly not a man.*

The hunters carrying the python had stopped as well. One of them came back to the redhead and asked something in the guttural tongue of the Mountain Men. The redhead pointed his great axe in Bret's general direction. The other man shrugged and began walking toward the fallen log. This Mountain Man saw the fire ants streaming from their hill and stepped back. If he'd stepped over the log, he'd discover the leafy mud there had eyes. He'd also get a sharp knife where all men dread. It was good he stopped just before the fallen log and loosened his furs.

The Mountain Man thoroughly watered the muddy leaves beyond the fallen log, before turning back to hoist the python. The little hunter's hands started shaking once the Mountain Men were out of sight. He violently smushed the fiery ants all over his body, and took a deep sip from his pouch. Fresh mud helped the bites. The little hunter let out a relieved sigh. The sun was high and strong to his right. Bret knew he was facing east.

It doesn't get much closer than that. That redheaded giant is a dangerous one. They almost had me, and they weren't even looking for me. Bret realized he was alive only because a man's bladder was too urgent to take another step.

Big scat. Big snake. Fire ants. Giants that pee on you. What a day, Bret thought. It isn't even noon. One thing for certain, I'm not taking a dip in this stream.

The little hunter had just made it to the crest of the little hill, when he sensed the second hunting team. He could hear them coming. Bret panned left, seeing the big cave Chief Sev had described. Even without the warning, there was something sinister about it. *They're still a ways off, moving with great skill, stalking slow, but coming. No chance. Not going in there, he thought.*

The little hunter took a deep breath and tested the wind.

Unclear. Are they stalking me or game? There's much better cover at the bottom of the hill. There's still time to move. It's better to be moving.

Movement gave him the feeling he still had control of his life. This was a partial illusion, if he thought it through. His body cooperated.

Bret crept to the bottom of the hill, into thicker growth. He sat back against a gnarled old willow. The little hunter soundlessly tuned in to the patterns of nearby bird calls. He heard something crashing onto the high grass of the little hill. He couldn't move much, but slowly turned his head for a peek. It was a large hairy boar. *They weren't stalking me*, he realized.

The exhausted little hunter was well hidden in the great purple birch before dusk. This tree on the big hill was a perfect hide. The creature comforts of water and a handful of berries had him feeling almost human again.

Thanks again, Chief Sev—everything's right where you said. I'm high up, safe, and nearly invisible within these folds. There's a commanding view of the Mountain Man village.

Bret knew he'd accomplished his mission mere moments after observing the village. *The Mountain Men are a beaten people. They've been devastated by the Sabretooth. War isn't even an option. They'd be lucky to survive the winter.*

The little hunter had never experienced the advanced stages of predation by a maneater. You could see it in the way the villagers walked. They almost stooped with the weight of fatalistic resignation on their shoulders. Their huts were in poor repair. They were all gaunt, pale, and thin, despite their towering size. It was also what you didn't hear. *Their children don't laugh or play. I doubt they have much food.*

Bret quickly formed his report, as their hunting teams returned before dusk.

I count eight hands worth of hunters. They aren't carrying the barbed war spears. Three teams came from the direction of the river. Given the distance to the river, I know when they left for home.

Even from this distance he could identify their leader. A powerful silver-haired man who walked with a pronounced limp. He was leading them all to their burial grounds for a Spirit Ceremony. The Mountain Men buried their dead in the ground with headstones. There were at least two rows of newer lightly colored headstones.

They'd prepared three fresh plots, one of which was smaller, for a child. Bret could see over the entire village and the burial grounds from the big hill. The entire village was at the ceremony, yet he saw someone running to a hut in the village. It was a smaller man, and he knelt at the door flap and seemed to be cutting. The man then raced back to the Spirit Ceremony.

This makes no sense. No one leaves a Spirit Ceremony. Bret realized they'd lost at least five hands' worth of people. The majority of these had to be the Sabretooth!

The Silver Hair was on his knees. He held a child's fur hat to his chest and kissed it before tossing it into the grave. The Sabretooth had taken his daughter. He rose and began screaming in fury as the grave was filled with dirt. The Mountain Men were all slashing cuts into their chests with knives, while the women tearfully pulled out strands of their hair. Bret had to look away for a while.

A tribe was a tribe. They all came together back in the village for the evening meal.

Bret thought, *All they have to eat is the python and the deer. This isn't enough food for so many people. The Silver Hair and many of the men aren't eating so the children could.*

As the great flames of their cooking fires danced in the darkness, the little hunter saw some sort of angry discussion in the village. The smaller man who'd snuck away from the Spirit Ceremony was giving an angry speech. He was pounding his chest and pointing east toward the Great Plains.

The Silver Hair stood up and drew a long line in the dirt with his ivory war axe. He crossed this line and turned back, facing his people. The red-haired giant was the first to cross. He stood shoulder to shoulder with the Silver Hair. All the Mountain Men followed suit, the entire village. The only one left was the angry small man. He grudgingly went last, crossing in silence.

Chapter Eleven
The Frog Spirit

"Truth is a lion, and lies are a hyena."
-Somali Proverb

THE YELLOW MOON ROSE that night with a windy breeze. Bret sensed, *The Sabretooth will come tonight. I'm grateful to be safely up this birch tree.* The Silver Hair had the same thought. He'd staked out four great torches next to the hut closest to the river. Then Bret watched the Mountain Man Chief sit cross-legged with his back resting against the hut. The great ivory war axe lay in his lap. The torch flames crackled and danced shadows and light in contrast to the vast darkness. Bret realized, *He's challenging the Sabretooth alone in the dark!*

The little hunter nodded grimly at the man's desperate courage. The Silver Hair wants to end this nightmare for his people. A lone wolf howl carried across the village from the direction of the little hill. It was a lonely, desolate sound on a bleak night. The sleepy Silver Hair howled back in response. Bret was tempted to respond in kind, but knew better.

The Silver Hair sprang to his feet, brandishing the war axe. Bret focused in. The red-haired giant stepped into the glow of the torches. It was clear he was trying to get the Chief to end this foolhardiness. When the Silver Hair refused, the giant simply planted his own war axe, and sat down next to him. *Brave men. You had to admire their courage.*

The little hunter realized he respected them. This didn't mean he wouldn't still do his duty for the People. If war came, either man would swiftly feel the deadly sting of Bret's spear, or a silent pair of knives through the throat. *Yet, they are brave men*, thought the little hunter.

The Mountain Men never knew how close death had come that night. A set of fiendish glowing eyes crouched in the darkness not twenty paces beyond the glow of the torches. The creature was crouched low and slow, slithering forward on its belly. The powerfully tawny haunches rippled with tension. The great cat had focused on the slumping Silver Hair. The Sabretooth's perfect night vision had detected the redheaded giant an instant before it charged the yawning Silver Hair. Two alert large Mountain Men were too dangerous. As skilled as the hunters were, the great cat at night was another level. Even Bret never knew how closely to his tree the great cat had crept on its way home in the moonlight.

The little hunter was utterly spent. The exertion and tension of the day's events had exhausted him. He double-checked the strap securing him to his branch. He suddenly felt very cold and lonely. *Why? I'll cross back to the People tomorrow. I must succeed. The Sabretooth will come for us next.*

The early gray daylight found the little hunter sipping water in his tree. The black crows by his tree were having an angry argument. Bret had figured out what the smallish Mountain Man was up to during the Spirit Ceremony. Bret could see the door to the Chief's hut swaying open in the dawn wind. The smaller man had sawed the door bindings down. The door to the sleeping Silver Hair's hut would have been wide open last night had the Sabretooth come. *This treacherous, angry little man had tried to murder the Silver Hair with the Sabretooth.*

Bret watched the Silver Hair dispatch three teams to watch the river. The remaining hunting teams set off as well. The Mountain Man Chief's team headed east.

Bret checked the clouds and wind. No rain today. The route home was simple.

Now I know when the river-watching teams head home. I'll follow the women and children who gather wood toward the river. Their chatter should cover my movements. I'll find a good tree near the river south of the bend. I'll wait for the river-watch teams to head home for dusk, then swim home. It's likely another night up a tree. A tree on our side of the river, though, is easier.

It was all going according to plan. By afternoon, the little hunter was perfectly hidden in a leafy hide close to the river. River frogs were croaking everywhere in the sun. Bret forced down a berry.

Then the little girl fell into the hide.

She'd been hunting frogs when the earth slipped beneath her. Bret sat there with his jaw open in shock. They stared at each other. The little Mountain Girl saw a strange creature caked in mud and leaves with a green face. He saw a freckled little face full of fear. *This was bad.*

The green frog in her hand ribbited. So did Bret. The hand that was flying to cover her mouth stopped and turned into a friendly wave hello. She looked at the frog, then Bret. He was instantly sitting like a frog too.

Bret knew he should cover her mouth, but stopped and ribbited more himself. He gave her his nicest ribbit and goofiest smile. *She seems more confused than scared.*

"Frosch?" the little girl asked.

The green-faced little hunter nodded emphatically. Then he offered her some berries.

He put his index finger to his nose in the shush sign. *I don't want to have to cover her mouth. If she screams, though, it's all over. The hunting teams are still between here and the river. She's too little to be missed for long. They'd all come looking for her.*

If a hunter had stumbled upon him, well, that was different. *This is an innocent child*. Bret made peace with the risk, even if it meant he died. Then he was calm.

The little hunter smiled at her. "The problem is I can't just leave you. I don't know if you are lost, and the Sabretooth is coming soon."

The little girl didn't understand any of this. She was very confused, but sensed whatever this green frog-looking creature was, it wouldn't eat her. Frogs can't talk, so he must be a Frog Spirit. Bret then heard faint women's voices from the west calling out, "Greta, Greta!"

Bret had to move. *They can't find the hide either.*

Bret said as tenderly as possible, "Greta, I'm taking you to Mama. I need you to be quiet."

He scooped up the child and gently covered her mouth. *She is confused but not scared*. Bret ran southwest toward a nearby grassy hill carrying Greta. He put her down at the summit facing north and pointed.

"Mama's coming," Bret said. "Greta, stay here. Stay here."

The little hunter scurried down the reverse slope of the little hill into some worn holly bushes. He cupped his hand to his mouth and screeched out the call of a peacock. "Miaooo, Miaooo!"

He watched uphill at Greta, until he was sure he heard the fussing Mountain Women running up the hill. Bret moved again, crawling quickly into another group of thorny bushes.

He saw a Mountain Woman pick her up. Greta was chattering away now and safe. The little hunter had time to be scared now. He threw up. *Young Greta will have some story to tell. She must've thought I was some big frog*, Bret chuckled inwardly. Then his hands started shaking again. Bret put his face in his hands and kneaded his temples. *I can smell the river. Almost home. Breathe. Focus. Move.*

The Mountain Woman was carrying Greta back to the others. The child was babbling something about a nice frog spirit. The odd thing was Greta had some dried berry juice on her cheeks, and a bit of smudged green paste on her shoulder. The Mountain Woman looked back over her shoulder at a slight rustle in the bushes headed back toward the river. *Whatever it was, it moved fast. Frog Spirit? No, it was just the wind.*

Bret knew the tree he was looking for. It was a magnificent old oak he'd seen from across the river. This tree was at the edge of a cliff that jutted out over the river. The little hunter finally had it in sight as the sun was hanging low in the sky. He sat close and perfectly silent, making certain he was alone. Then he was up high in the branches well beyond the Sabretooth's reach. He could even dive into the river from here if needed. It was so quiet and peaceful. Bret was very tempted to just swim across now. The little hunter gritted his teeth and remembered his discipline. It was still too light out, though his eyelids were heavy.

The little hunter thought, *Why is it in war you can never sleep when you get the chance, but it's so hard to stay awake when you need to? No, this isn't war unless I screw it up.*

Two Mountain Men passed right below his tree headed home before dusk. It was just a feeling—he couldn't see, smell, or hear anything unusual. Yet the little hunter's hairs rose on the back of his neck. He knew better than to dismiss this feeling. Then he sensed rather than saw a faint shrub move below

They are running late, thought the little hunter. *It'll catch them before they make the village. Hurry, boys*, he thought. Bret then realized he knew the Sabretooth was close. *I'm not going anywhere tonight.*

The great cat was stalking this hunting team on the sly. It also passed right under his tree. *How can something so big move that stealthily? There's no way it could sense me. The wind is with me.*

Bret was hidden well, perfectly still high up in thick leaves. He was wrong. It still found him.

Bret got lucky later, because in his exhaustion he made a deadly mistake that night. The fatigued little hunter had relaxed a bit with home in sight. He'd moved down to a more comfortable branch for the night. He was drowsy, and misjudged the distance in the darkness. This new branch was broader and sturdy, but wasn't high enough. The cat had sensed him earlier, and returned just before dawn.

It was silently creeping up the back of the tree, when it slipped. The Sabretooth was in the act of reaching around the huge tree trunk for a sleeping Bret. It almost had him. The girth of the ancient tree trunk saved him. Something primal woke the little hunter to the danger in the darkness. The drowsy hunter heard the faintest scratching sound on the trunk below and behind. He suddenly felt an instant of sharp padded fur on his chest, then a falling roar behind and below. Something heavy and growling thudded through the branches into the ground below. Bret dove straight off the branch into the dark river.

The plucky little hunter was back in the village by midmorning with a big smile, a bigger tiger paw scratch right across his chest, and an even bigger story. He sat noisily eating and drinking everything in sight. The boys brought him a bunch of fresh cherries they had just picked.

He'd reported the mission details to Chief Sev, and the Elders. *No war. The Sabretooth will be coming for us too.* They were shocked at what the Sabretooth had done to the Mountain Men. Chief Sev decided the hidden rock path under the waterfall might prove very useful.

Bret put down an enormous piece of venison, and wiped the grease from his mouth. The village medicine man carefully applied a paste of mushrooms and healing herbs to the claw scratch. It wasn't deep, but extended all the way across the little hunter's chest.

The People were genuinely thrilled to see the little warrior again. Leif grabbed his shoulder warmly. Bron shook hands in silent respect. Emil just gave Bret a big hug.

The little hunter was finishing his story for the People: "Then I swam back to our side, and ran past at least two sprinting deer on the way home!"

The People laughed at this. Bret looked down at his chest, reflecting, "It wasn't my time, I guess."

Papa teased. "Was that scar really necessary, or are you just trying to impress all the women.... Oh, this little thing...just a scratch from a man-eating Sabretooth!"

Bret just shrugged and belched. He tapped his chest with his usual buoyant bluster.

"I got this this morning. This cat is...devilishly cunning. I've never seen anything like it. Chief Sev's directions were perfect. The Mountain Men are living a nightmare. With the night comes a relentless beast which preys on your loved ones. The men can't stop it, no matter what they try. Their Silver Hair is crazy but brave. I wish I had one of your venom darts, Emil. That might have ended this nightmare for all of us. This was a close thing. I made so many mistakes we can learn from, Emil. I got very lucky more than once."

The little hunter addressed the Chief, "Cloud is what has kept us safe so far. The snows may hinder it, but eventually this wicked cat will come for us too."

Papa brought back Bret's throwing stick and weapons—there were two new darts capped with small tied rawhide covers. These were the venom darts. In addition to the caps, they had three slight notches carved into the stalk to identify them. He told Bret, "I showed this to the hunters. Most think its bad snake magic and will anger the snake spirits."

Bret scoffed, "More for us. We won't be able to get more venom darts until the spring."

Papa addressed the hunters in a calm, even voice.

"We shouldn't wait, let's go after the Sabretooth at dawn. We should use all of our hunting teams at once, as well as the Mountain Men. We'll use all but two of the teams to funnel and push the Sabretooth toward the river with smoke, noise, and fire. The older boys can help too. The top two teams will be waiting by the river. If somehow the cat escapes into the river, we know the Mountain Men are waiting on the other side. Cloud will help locate the beast."

Chief Sev nodded in approval then raised an eyebrow. "Will the wolf do this?"

"He'll listen to me if Emil tells him to," Papa stated.

He saw the Chief shaking his head. "No, Spearmaker, we are lost without your spears and darts."

Papa added, "Yes, we are lost. Chief, you've seen what this cat can do. It's not hunting. The law says the Spearmaker may fight to defend the village. Emil is too young and Cloud may not obey anyone else. We must end this terror."

"Give me your word once the smoke drive starts you stay well behind the driving teams," Chief Sev said. He turned to Bret. "You and Leif will lead the killing teams."

The little hunter's blunt reply surprised them all.

"You honor me, Chief, and no disrespect, Spearmaker, but this plan won't work on the Shaitan that is this cat. The best way to sort this out, Chief, is simple. Cloud, Aash, and myself quietly stalk it down using the venom darts. I know this cat's mind. Cloud is the best hunter in the village, and the Spearmaker...well, he's just too ugly for the Sabretooth to eat."

"No chance," was the Chief's instant reply. "With you two dead, then I'm the ugliest man in the village."

The hunters laughed darkly at this, which briefly cut through the thick tension hanging over their heads. Bret nodded. "Understood. Let Leif and Bron lead their hunting teams. I'll go with them, but I hunt best alone."

Chief Sev ordered Bret to sleep until dawn. The entire plan was made clear to all the hunters. It was a maximum effort to kill the Sabretooth.

That night in the Gher, Emil asked about bravery. "Papa, is Bret the bravest hunter of the People? How can I be brave, Papa?"

Papa answered slowly. He knew the risks Bret had taken.

"Bravery is doing ordinary things in extraordinary circumstances. All of our men are trained in the hunting arts. What makes Bret a hero, is he was able to do his duty despite knowing there was a very good chance it was a one-way trip. The difficulty of infiltrating past skilled hunters, not to mention the dangers of the cat, are above and beyond most of us. He was able to do this less due to his considerable skill, than his love for the People.”

“You could’ve done it too, Papa,” voiced Emil, “that’s why Bret asked you that you two sort this out.”

Aash ran a hand through his son’s hair. *There is nothing like the faith of a child to keep us safe.*

“Your opa the Eagle Feather could have done it.” Papa winked. “Bret asked for me mainly because I’m the only one who laughs at his jokes. He also knows I’d be stubborn and stupid enough to go. Sleep, Babo—something tells me tomorrow will be a very long day.”

Chapter Twelve
The Sabretooth

"You don't go searching for bones in a lion's den."
-Somali Proverb

DAWN BROUGHT A CHILLY blanket of thick fog over the valley. The usual warm amber rays faintly peeked through the clouds. The white wolf was sniffing Sabretooth spore on the dew-caked ground. Cloud glared up the skyline with low growls. There was a final quiet moment before the din as the wind cut through the fog. Papa took in the fresh crisp smell of maple. Beautiful hues of red, yellow, and orange autumn leaves painted in patches as far as the eye could see. *It's so hard to imagine death is so close amidst such beauty*. Yet it surely was.

Chief Sev gave the command as the line of hunters lit their torches. The line of men broke into high-pitched yells and screams. The frosty breath escaped their mouths as they clanged their spears together, marching up toward the hill caves. Papa released Cloud, and the beating line of hunters followed as a long broad wave to the caves.

The Sabretooth reacted instantly to the sounds and smoke. He sensed the white wolf and hated man smell. The cat let out a bloodcurdling roar in challenge, which resonated ominously through the hills.

By the river, Bret and the hunting teams were spread apart and waiting with throwing sticks and heavy spears at the ready. They could vaguely hear the clamor from over the hills. They watched smoke from the line of torches swirl up the hill into the fog. No one missed hearing the cat's response. Then it was eerily quiet, but for the whistling wind.

Leif expertly positioned the teams. He was the strongest hunter of the People and knew exactly where the cat would likely come from. Bret climbed up a large boulder and tossed up a handful of dirt to gauge the wind. He loaded a venom dart and shook the tension from his hands. They were ready. *It'll be any moment now*. Peals of thunder suddenly began murmuring through the heavy clouds. Bret shielded his eyes from the swirling wind and scanned the darkening horizon. The teams laughed as the crazy little hunter called out, "Here, kitty kitty!"

They waited, waited, and waited. The cat never came. Bret thought, *Well, at least it's not raining*. Then as if on cue, a single raindrop fell as sparks of an old familiar fear shot up the back of his spine. The little hunter asked himself an awful question. Then he knew. A hard rain fell.

Bret yelled at Leif, "Stay in position! Keep blocking off the waterfall tunnel!" He began sprinting uphill, cursing as thunder boomed again loudly through the fog.

The line of beating hunters came to a narrow ridge leading up to a large rocky cave. Cloud was very agitated by the cave. Chief Sev halted the hunters, pointing his heavy spear at the cave entrance.

"That's its lair," Papa uttered, "Cloud would tell us if he was close."

The first seed of a very dark thought began creeping into the back of Papa's mind. The Chief led the hunters into the cave without result. He emerged moments later with the shocked pale face of a man who's seen a ghost. He just pointed back up at the cave. Papa and Cloud bounded past them up into the cave. The glimmering torchlight revealed a dark, damp cave. It reeked of cat urine and dead carrion as expected. The shock was the floor was covered in a thick harvest of human skeletons. Papa counted at least a dozen skulls. *Tigers don't do this*. Was this a message? He calmed his mind, reminding himself, *It's just a cat*. Cloud raised a leg and urinated in contempt. Papa smirked a dark smile and did the same. They made their way back down to Chief Sev.

Cloud had stopped tracking as the cold raindrops dampened the foggy air. The white wolf had lost the scent. He paused and lifted his head up, looking back to lock eyes with Papa. Thunder rumbled from the clouds above. Cloud began barking wildly and raced across the line of hunters downhill. Papa followed, immediately yelling out, "Get back to the village!"

The Sabretooth sprang into the village with a set of savage growls that froze the blood. It was in a bloody killing frenzy. The first victims were two elders, who were sitting at the edge of the village talking and smoking their pipes. The cat slashed one across the face with a thunderous paw stroke. It tore the other's throat open as he futilely stabbed at it with his pipe. The entire village instantly became a swirling mass of confused and terrified women, children, and elders. Some were running for weapons, others were trying to escape the fire, most were just running.

A woman fleeing in terror tripped over the basket holding the grease from all the hunted game. It fell into the fire, releasing thick, engulfing black smoke into the foggy rain. The village was now a dark, blazing hell of screams, roars, and terror. The Sabretooth tore into the nearest Gher. There was a young mother within who died saving her infant. She sprang at the cat with a hysterical scream, striking it in the face with a burning firebrand of kindling. It ripped her to shreds. The cat had a badly seared eye and recoiled back out of the Gher with a high-pitched snarl.

A gray-haired elder confused by the smoke ran right into the Sabretooth by accident. It turned, snapping at her. She opened the flap of the nearest Gher and dove in. Lulu was startled to see a screaming old woman suddenly sprawling through their Gher flap. Mama was backed up inside as far as possible, with a big knife raised and Emil behind her. A thunderous roar shook the entire Gher. In a flash something powerful yanked the hysterical Elder right back out. Mama slashed open the back of the Gher, grabbed Emil and ran through. Behind her she could hear the dull sickening crunch of snapping bones.

The cat released the limp old woman and bellowed as it rolled its scalded face in the dirt. It came to its feet snarling and swirled to chase panicked villagers. The Sabretooth now faced a small group of women, children, and a teen boy. Mama and Emil were part of this group. The teen charged with a heavy spear and a battle cry, while the women reached for fallen torches. The Sabretooth swatted the spear aside and killed the teen with a massive bite to the chest. The mother, now closest to the cat, handed her infant to Lulu to take him and run. Mama ran for the trees, carrying a screaming Emil over her shoulder and the baby in the other arm. The third woman followed carrying the other children. The infant's mother made her desperate stand with a greasy flaming torch and a dull knife. The cat was more cautious now as the heat from the torch increased pain from its burned eye. The woman was determined to die well and swirled the burning torch around the cat's face in primal fury.

This desperate standoff was ended by the deep sound of rapidly approaching wolf growls. The Sabretooth knew the wolf and hunters were moments away. It turned and tore low and fast out of the village, headed for the river. Cloud went straight for Emil's scent, showing up just as Mama, Emil, and the baby reached the trees. The rain made climbing slippery. Mama had Emil up on a branch and was handing him the baby. Lulu heard growls behind her. She twirled, drawing her knife, only to see Cloud's effortless gait emerging through the fog. Mama dropped to her knees to give the white wolf a relieved hug as it licked her face. Cloud stayed there to guard them as she climbed up after Emil.

Papa was the first hunter to reach the smoking village. He saw their torn Gher was empty and his heart sank. In the confusion more hunters arrived and all were now searching the smoke for the cat. None had seen it leave amidst the fog, smoke, and screams. Papa came upon the mother who had stood down the Sabretooth; she was down on one knee now, trembling and shaking. He asked for Lulu. The mother pointed to the trees behind the village. Papa slipped in the muddy rain, then sprinted past her.

Bret was hurtling downhill as fast as his legs could carry him. The village was covered in a ghastly cloud of smoke and thick sideways rain. The little hunter tripped. He fell into a thorny bush, cursing the muddy earth. The rain and mud had extinguished his torch.

He could see a few hunters reaching the smoke and heard wails and screams, but no roars. Bret wiped the mud out of his eyes and was picking thorns out of his forearms when his peripheral vision saw slight movement. A slinking tawny blur streaked across the base of the next hill into thick forest. *It's headed back for the river.* Bret turned back to follow it, screaming a hoarse, dry-throated warning to the hunters by the river.

At the river, Leif could see smoke rising from the direction of the village. These hunters knew the Sabretooth must have hit the village. They forced themselves to stay in place by the boulders blocking the river. Yet their minds were actively thinking of their loved ones in the village. It was too much; all but two couldn't wait any longer and ran for the village. The dark rain was increasing, putting out their torches, and making visibility poor.

Leif was brushing his long rain-swept hair out of his face when he heard a shocked scream. The cat landed on Bron right behind him. It'd pounced on him from atop the nearest boulder behind them. The Sabretooth instantly snapped mighty Bron's neck before bounding off the trail toward the river. Leif missed the cat with his heavy spear and crashed after it into the bushes with his war club. As he retrieved the spear, Leif saw movement to his right. Bret noiselessly stepped off a trail beneath him. Both the largest and the smallest hunter in the village were chasing the cat now. Bret began grimly chanting his war mantra. "Now I am become Death, the destroyer of worlds."

The trail came to an imposing fork protruding in the rocky trail right before the river. The blustering white water of the river drowned out all other sounds. A pair of narrow trails ringed a series of large granite boulders. One was pitch dark, while the other had intermittent specks of light and shadow dancing reflections across the surface. A silent look passed between Bret and Leif. Both knew it was foolish to separate, but there was no time. Leif's hair fell into his face again. He shrugged back a toothy grin and took the more dangerous trail. Bret nodded, taking the other.

Bret could hear the roar of the river around the next bend in the trail. He knew the Sabretooth wanted to make the hidden rock tunnel. Leif had positioned well to cut that direction off.

The Sabretooth knew the men were close and saw it was trapped on the edge of a slippery rocky ledge high above the river. It turned to see a huge, wild-looking man with a heavy spear. Leif was a brave man. He was going to end this murderous cat once and for all. The strongest hunter of the People lunged at the Sabretooth with the ancient war cry. With an infernal roar it pounced in reply. Leif was almost on the cat when he slipped on the rainy rock surface. The Sabretooth, faster than the eye could see, smacked the stumbling hunter's spear down.

Bret rounded the corner just in time to see glowing yellow eyes and the cat's monstrous head take Leif's entire head in its gaping black jaws. Large, jagged ivory canines effortlessly decapitated the powerful hunter with a sickening crunch. The

Sabretooth then violently shook his body the way a big snake thrashes a small mouse. The little hunter advanced on this horror.

Bret's sudden stealthy arrival startled the great cat, who spat out Leif's head and leapt back to the edge of the precipice. The little hunter balanced himself carefully on the rain-splattered bloody surface. A powerful venom dart caught the cat, creasing its flank deeply. The Sabretooth snarled, snapping at the wound, and then slipped itself, slowly falling backwards off the edge. Bret drew his knife and advanced with the final venom dart in the other hand. He caught a glare of pure primeval malevolence from the beast. A look which slowly devolved, turning into full panic. The big cat tried futilely to pull itself back over, chipping and scraping its front claws into the slippery rock. Then it was gone over the side. Bret saw its body crash into the raging river far below with a swirling splash, and get swept under the frothy current.

The roar of the river was deafening, but Bret thought he heard echoes of distinct cheers rising through the mist. He looked over to see two burly Mountain Men on the opposite bank raising their spears in joyous salute to the little hunter. A gust of wind sprayed a fine river mist over the edge of the ledge. Bret retrieved Leif's spear, promising, "We'll be back for you soon, brother," as he made his way back to the village. It had stopped raining and scattered beams of sunlight were now tentatively burning through the fog.

Life was hard for the People. The village showed remarkable resilience considering the circumstances. The fires were out and order had been restored. Chief Sev was leading work parties as the exhausted little hunter entered the village. Bret's eyes met Papa's. Emil was sitting cuddled between his parents and ran over to give his mentor a hug.

Papa answered Bret's unspoken question. "Bad, very bad, four dead, twice as many wounded, three critically." Chief Sev and the returned hunters wearily approached the little hunter.

Bret preempted, "Six dead, the cat got Leif and Bron." He told them of Leif's courage and fate.

"I hit it solidly with a venom dart after it killed Leif. It fell off the edge of the high cliffs into the river, and I saw it sucked under. That fall alone should have killed it, or the venom, or the river, or all three. But I can't be sure. It's all enough to make you old."

"I've never seen anything like it," grimaced the little hunter, "that creature was pure evil."

Chapter Thirteen
Lions, Tigers, and Bears

"The friendship of the great is fraternity with lions."
-Italian Proverb

THE VILLAGE WOKE TO a heavy stillness the next morning. The People knew death, but it was too quiet. Everyone was grateful to have survived the Sabretooth. Each felt some pangs of guilt for not doing more when so many of their loved ones would never stir again. The Spirit Ceremony was the place to stem the small hidden river of tears in everyone's eyes. In the meantime, the meat supply was low. Winter was coming. Four damaged Ghers and the grease supply had to be replaced. Chief Sev wisely sensed all this, and gently but firmly put them all to work.

Papa was finally putting the finishing touches on Bret's obsidian knife when the little hunter hobbled over in greeting. Bret was limping from a twisted ankle, pale in appearance, and in obvious need of rest. Papa knew better than to chide him. The exhaustion and stress of the past few days would have put most men down. Carnivora often have decayed flesh residue under their claws, and resulting scratch wounds often resulted in deadly infection. The People had learned which plants and crushed mushrooms to apply, but even then, some infection was likely.

Bret's scratches itched and the usually merry little hunter was in a sour mood. Then Papa handed him his obsidian knife. "This is magnificent," Bret yelled jubilantly.

The serrated obsidian blade was perfectly shaped, resembling a large oval leaf. Papa had used dark birch for the handle with a slight curve for powerful thrusting and cutting. The sheath was tan buckskin with a flying fish pattern carved into it.

Papa observed, "That obsidian is the best I've seen. Is there more where you found it?"

Bret recounted, "Emil found it in a rock bed by the fishing spot. I'll take you, Spearmaker. I'm tired of sleep and not allowed to hunt or scratch these infernal scars today."

Papa mentioned, "I'm still thinking about all those bones that cat kept in the cave. Some of those were of the People. We should at least bury them properly."

Emil was begging to tag along, so he and Cloud accompanied the two men. It seemed like the forest was letting out a collective sigh of relief that the Sabretooth was gone. The sun was back and shooting golden lances of light through the trees. Blackbirds were pleasantly arguing with red squirrels, and there was plenty of deer sign again.

At the cat's cave, they cautiously lit torches. Cloud led them in. It was dank, dingy, and ominous.

Bret took in the ghostly layer of bleached cracked bones. "I see what you mean, Spearmaker," he mumbled grimly, "if I'd have seen this first, I may not have gone after it."

The little hunter pointed to the walls and a smoke hole in the ceiling, "Men lived here once."

Papa had missed this. He swept aside a thick layer of cobwebs and held the torch to a wall. The flames illuminated wall carvings telling of men and animals. The ancient images were of hunting and fighting. There were mammoth, tigers, and strong spirits too. It looked like they had throwing sticks as well, though with a severe bend to them. Emil peered intensely at the wall as if in a trance.

Papa pointed. "These men had strong spirits. Look how that large lightning from the sky is helping them hunt mammoth in the woods."

Emil felt the dark cave was sinister. He was pleased when they left it. They respectfully buried the bones and left for the rock bed. Bret's slight limp gave them plenty of time to talk.

Cloud bounded up ahead, sniffing intensely at fresh spoor on the ground. Bret knelt wincing in the dirt. He shifted the weight off his sore ankle. "Wild dogs, a big, dangerous pack."

The dirt trail ended in a damp grassy area which extended into a narrow rocky chapparal. There was a gorge on one side and sloping high plains on the other. Cloud kept tracking in the direction of the grassy plains.

Bret asked, "Emil, which way did the dogs go—how would you know if Cloud wasn't telling us?"

Emil thought really hard. The tracks ended with the dirt. There were no animal sounds or wind.

"I don't know," he replied dejectedly to his mentor.

Bret took a knee next to the boy, voicing, "Good, it's smart to say so when you don't know something. Many men can't do this. It's often not the things we don't know that cause problems; it's the things we know which aren't true." Papa nodded in full agreement.

Bret pointed at the dew on the grass. "There's still dew on the grass ahead toward the plain. See here, there's much less in the direction of the gorge. The pack's feet soaked the dew off the grass that way. A big pack of hungry wild dogs is a nasty thing—we'll go the other way."

Papa whistled inwardly at Bret's mastery. Most experienced trackers can read sign. Bret barely did. Instead the little hunter always looked ahead, already knowing the animal's path.

Emil thought it was so easy when you knew what to look for and looked away embarrassed. Bret sensed this and smiled. "Your opa taught me this. It's only easy when a great tracker teaches you."

Emil proclaimed, "I've never seen wild dogs. They aren't that big, right?"

Papa responded, "They are very cunning, hard to find, and the smartest animal in the forest. A pack of wild dogs will hunt anything in the forest except a mammoth. They prefer deer, but will even attack and eat tigers or panthers, though at great cost. You are right, Babo—they aren't that big but have powerful jaws. They are smart and hunt as a team. Just like us."

Bret cracked, "Why does a hunter have to be big to be dangerous, Emil?"

Papa and Emil got the little hunter's joke.

"What is the most dangerous game?" Emil asked.

Papa and Bret looked at each other for a second and replied in unison, "That depends."

This was a long topic of discussion as they gathered obsidian from the rock bed.

Bret added some obsidian stone to the pouch and began.

"Everything we hunt is dangerous and can kill you. It's true for mammoth down to the little gazelles. Every hunter of the People is brave. For me, it's deer and bear. We lose more hunters to deer, especially in mating season, than any other animal. I think it's because deer aren't predators. We aren't as cautious and forget how powerful their hooves and horns can be.

"A bear has no weakness. It's crafty with good hearing and eyesight, and their sense of smell is unmatched in the forest. Despite their size they can catch a deer over a short distance. We don't hunt bear unless we have to. At spear range they are just too dangerous. A big cat's nose isn't much better than ours. If you get a good spear into a cat, it will go down. As powerful as they are, a big cat is much thinner skinned, with less fat for protection. Bears often steal our kills. At close range a big bulky bear can absorb three spears and still wipe out a four-man hunting team before you can blink. Though this might be different with your papa's darts."

Papa added, "Wind discipline is crucial in bear country. The easiest way to see a bear is to kill a deer or elk. A huge ill-tempered Grizzly will smell it and come take it from you."

Bret chuckled darkly and knowingly at this, and Papa went on.

"Bears are very territorial and mark trees with claws. This tells you when you are in bear country and how big the bear is. Deer is important bear food, but berries are most important. Be very alert around berry bushes, especially late in the fall. All bears are very unpredictable. I surprised a massive rough-looking bear once near a berry bush. I was up the nearest tree in a flash, but it was running away from me just as fast. Another time, though, a little black bear stalked and charged my whole hunting team. We don't hunt them unless we have no choice."

Papa thought on it. "Panthers and mammoth are the most dangerous to me."

Emil was surprised. "Why not a tiger?"

Bret nodded at Papa's answer and responded.

"The big cats are dangerous in different ways. We aren't usually their natural prey despite being a lot easier to kill than anything else they hunt. I think it's because we smell so bad to them! They are ambush predators, built for power more than chasing down gazelle on the plains. Both panthers and tigers have the best night eyes and hearing. You will never see a panther during the day, and a tiger rarely, except for a maneater.

"Both are incredibly stealthy, but a tiger is more predictable in some ways. A tiger, for example, has a certain beat or territory it sticks to. If you see a tiger track, at some point the tiger will be back in that area. It's different for panthers. The danger of a panther is it's even stealthier and never completely loses its fear of man. A panther will always let you pass and silently ambush you from the rear. It kills using all four paws and its fangs. It's much smaller than a tiger. It tries for a bite to the back of the neck. Unlike a tiger, a panther is completely unpredictable.

"A tiger, on the other hand, is much braver. It can ambush you too, but will also announce itself with a growl and charge you. A tiger kills by snapping the neck. It can also kill you with one swipe of a paw. A tiger is much more powerful. If you see the charge you have a chance to get a spear into it. You will never see a panther. It's just like your papa says. Most big cats don't want us, but some decide they do. It's most dangerous in the darkest nights of a new moon."

Emil asked, "What about mammoth, is it because they are so big?"

Papa answered, thinking back to a winter hunt.

"Yes, they travel in large, powerful herds. They run much faster than you think and are relentless when provoked. Its trunk can smell you from very far away and it will chase you half the day and kill you four times. A mammoth can smack you with its trunk, or grab you with it and smash you into every tree in the area. It can stomp you into the dirt, and we haven't mentioned the tusks. Their thick hide is also very hard to get a spear through. We hunt them with fire and drive them off cliffs unless we can isolate one. Otherwise it's sure death."

Bret chimed in with an observation that only hunters know.

"The amazing thing about a mammoth is how often you can't see them. Anything that size should be easy to spot. Somehow, they just know how to move using the land and trees for cover. I've stood close to a mammoth in heavy brush. I watched it walk from tall grass behind thorny trees. I knew it was there but couldn't see it! It sure smelled me, though, when the wind changed. It chased me for half a day. It took every trick I knew and some luck to get away. It's also true they have great memories. A mammoth herd will see a trap and rarely fall for it the next migration.

"Emil, no two animals are alike—what we are teaching you is based on good experience. It's all only true, until it isn't. Out here everything bites and only food runs!"

Papa paused as old memories returned to him. "There is something else. In some ways, mammoth seem the most human of all the forest animals. It's something in their eyes. Emil, your opa would not hunt mammoth later in life."

Bret and Emil both turned and focused on Papa with acute interest as he continued.

"The People were suffering a brutally harsh winter with little food left. They saw a small mammoth herd on the plains headed for a small gully. The meat was worth the risk. Our hunters beat the mammoths to the gully and dug some deep pits in the snow just off the path. We covered them with shrubs and branches. As the herd passed our hunters began imitating Sabretooth calls and using torches and smoke to try to panic the herd off the path. It was starting to work, except a big Old Bull mammoth knew this trick.

"He was trumpeting loudly for the herd to stay on the path. He turned back and stood his ground, ferociously blocking the trail from behind. Opa said we wanted no part of him. There was then a weighty silence to the frosty air which was suddenly pierced by a bleating cry off to the side.

"A frightened young calf had panicked and fallen into one of the hidden pits. All the People had to do now was wait—there would be plenty of meat. Opa thought the herd had no choice but to leave the calf and held the hunters back out of danger.

"The Old Bull saw this and ran over to the pit, looking down at the crying calf. His gaze swept back over the hunters and to his herd now escaping safely out of the gully. The Old Bull let out a thunderous huffing bellow. Every hunter shook in fear of his charge.

"Then the mammoth turned and slid slowly down into the pit. He gingerly picked up the squirming calf and lifted it over the edge of the pit. The Old Bull smacked it on the backside so it would sprint to catch the herd. The calf was safe now, but the Old Bull knew he was trapped.

"The Eagle Feather was deeply touched by the Old Bull's leadership and sacrifice. He said, 'Those old venerable eyes knew exactly what it was doing.' This meat saved the People that winter, but your opa never hunted mammoth again."

Emil had moist eyes. Bret also looked away, as if quietly picking something out of his eyes.

"I never heard that story. Thank you," remarked the little hunter.

The stony rock bed had yielded a bountiful supply of obsidian. Papa's flint pouch was filled with enough of the sharp volcanic stones to make eight to ten new spears as well as a few knifes. One glossy oblong piece was almost as good for a hunting knife as Bret's.

Emil peppered them both with questions on the way back to the village. Cloud flushed a flock of birds out of a little wood off the trail and the boy found a few eggs for his pouch. They all marveled again at the abundance of fresh game sign around them.

Emil asked, "Papa, why do we send hunting teams in the four directions every day?"

Papa's reply was slow in coming and thought out.

"Babo we never know how the game animals move or migrate. After a while there isn't enough game in an area and we have to move the village to follow the game. So, it's best to hunt in all directions."

Emil responded, "Yes, Papa, but we haven't moved the village in a long time. Is this because where we are now is good for game and water?"

Both men nodded in agreement, and they could see a tentative question on the boy's mind.

"Papa, because of the Sabretooth, the People didn't hunt or go near the Mountain River for a full four days. Look how many game animals are here now. What if, instead of hunting in all four directions every day, we only hunted in two or three directions? Wouldn't the animals in the quiet directions for a couple of days lose some fear of being hunted? They'd all come back like we are seeing in the river direction today? We might not have to move the village away from a good spot like we have now."

"That's a very good question, young buck," whistled Bret appreciatively.

Papa thought this made sense too. It was so obvious when you thought it through. He made a point to bring this up to Chief Sev back in the village.

Chapter Fourteen
The Mistake

"Better one day as a lion than a hundred as a sheep."
-Spartan Proverb

IT WAS A PERFECT day for the Spirit Ceremony. The sky was robin's egg blue and there wasn't a single cloud in sight. A slight aromatic wind wafted faint vestiges of sweet maple and juniper into the village. Robins, cardinals, and blackbirds serenaded the young sun from nearby trees.

Chief Sev addressed the People.

"We are the Auroch People. The Sky Spirits look down on us just as they did our ancestors. They sent the first Auroch. There is a time for everything, a time to live, a time to die for every creature. Some of us live to be old and gray, others see but a single winter. It's all written in the stars. All of this is beyond our control. We only control our thoughts and actions.

"I'm so proud to be Chief of the People. We lost good people, strong hunters, young mothers, wise elders, and bright children. All were taken far too soon, far too fast. All bravely died in service to the People.

"Leif and Bron died fighting the Sabretooth as warriors should. Kara, a young mother, sacrificed herself to save her baby. Arik, a young man, charged the cat like the brave hunter he soon hoped to be so others could escape. The three Elders, Jun, Max, and Eli, went down fighting as well. We honor them today, and send their bodies up to the Sky Spirits to watch over us. We grieve for them. We never forget them and we go on. If your heart is heavy, think of how blessed we are such People lived. Lulu will lead us in the People's song as we send our honored into the sky."

Papa was holding Emil's hand as Mama led the People's song. The wooden pyres were lit as the hazy blue smoke circled lazily up to be received by the Sky Spirits. The village went back to work. Hunting teams went out for game. The women continued to work on the damaged Ghers. There weren't very many bird eggs for the boys to find this time of year.

Kilan, Mats, Lars, and Emil were watching the determined bustle around them.

Lars ranted, "We should hunt eggs, but there are none. The hunters are looking for game. We should do something to help the people too."

Emil recalled, "I was by the Bear River yesterday too. The fish run is over, but there were plenty just lying there on the shore or in shallow pools. I just didn't have a basket."

Kilan and Mats thought it would be a great idea to take baskets and bring the People back fresh silver-scaled fish.

Emil shook his head. "It's too late in the season. My papa says the bears are too dangerous before their winter sleep. They would never let us go alone, and all the adults are busy today."

Lars blurted back, "We will be really quick! Maybe the bears are already asleep, and we'd have Cloud with us! We could all be great heroes like Bret."

Emil shook his head. "The rule is no one leaves the village without telling someone first. We shouldn't go to Bear River. My papa said all the bears are there gorging on fish and berries."

Lars was adamant, "We even won't go by any berry bushes! If the fish are just lying trapped or close to shore like you said, we can really help. Besides, bears aren't dangerous unless you scare them when they're with their cubs. Cloud can smell them first."

Mats bragged, "No bear can catch me. Emil, you are just scared. I'm taking a basket like a real hunter and getting fish for the People. You can stay here and help the girls fix the Ghers, Emil."

"We have to let someone know we are going at least," pleaded Emil, but no one heard him but Cloud.

Kilan and Lars grabbed baskets and followed Mats. Emil knew it was wrong. He grabbed a basket and told a little girl from the village where they were going. Emil and Cloud ran out to follow the boys before she could answer.

Papa and Bret were chipping the new obsidian into spear points. The sun was at its highest point in the sky. Papa had mentioned the idea of rotating hunting sectors to Chief Sev. His only hesitation was the People might be blind from approaching enemies in quiet sectors.

Bret, with no patience for crafting a spearpoint, had a thought.

"True, but as we saw on the other hand, there'd be so much more game to hunt. We could remain in a favorable area like we have now. There's plenty of game here, good water from two rivers, and we can see any approaches to the village. Maybe we just avoid one sector at a time instead of two. We could even scout around the edge of a sector while leaving it open."

A little girl named Shala brought them cold meat, berries, and water. The men thanked her initiative. Papa realized he hadn't seen Emil or heard Cloud barking since the Spirit Ceremony. He asked Shala if Emil and the boys were out picking eggs.

Shala looked away quickly. The little girl had a conflicted look on her face.

Papa went on, "Shala, what aren't you telling me? Are the boys in the village? This is very important."

Shala rolled her eyes. "No, Mira told me the stupid boys went to get fish at the Bear River, with Cloud."

Papa and Bret were the only two hunters left in the village. They both shared an incredulous look. Then Papa's voice had a trace of alarm: "Lulu knows the bears are too dangerous by the river now. She'd never take them?"

"No," said Shala, "she is helping fix Ghers. I just saw Emil and Cloud leave alone."

Papa and Bret dropped their food, grabbed their weapons, and began sprinting for the river. She could hear the Spearmaker praying as he ran. Bret was loudly screaming words she had heard but didn't know what they meant. Everyone knew Bret was the fastest runner of the People. Shala saw he was two lengths behind the Spearmaker, as she lost sight of them in the woods.

The riverbank was full of pink and silver salmon squirming and flopping in the sandy shallows. There was fresh bear sign everywhere. This smaller river was called the Bear River for good reason. Emil knelt at the water's edge, nervously filling his basket with the speckled fish. The far bank held even more of the grounded silver-scaled fish. The shallow stream sparkled in the sunlight.

Kilan pointed to a massive bear claw mark high up a tree trunk, admitting, "You're right, Emil—we'd better be quick.

You stay here. We'll grab all those fish on the other side and leave fast."

Emil pleaded, "Let's just go now! The trees are too close to the water on the other side. We are downwind. If there are bears in that dark grove, Cloud can't smell them!"

The other three boys' eyes just saw all the fresh fish flopping in front of them and didn't listen. They hurriedly splashed across to the other side. Emil stayed put and focused on filling his basket as fast as possible. He tried to breathe through the dreadful feeling coming over him.

Kilan was grabbing a trapped fish from the stream when he heard a twig snap behind him. He had that eerie sinking feeling you get when something is watching you. The boy shielded his brow from the glaring sunlight while looking back into the sage underbrush. Nothing. Kilan reached back into the stream for a big speckled fish. There was a nearly imperceptible sound behind him. The sound of a heavy padded foot. Kilan wouldn't have heard the sound even if it wasn't muffled by the flowing stream. The bad feeling was stronger. He knew it was time to go. Somehow, he was suddenly, inexplicably in the shade. Cloud growled from the opposite bank, just as Kilan saw the reflection of a colossal silvertip bear standing right behind him in the stream.

The boys all screamed as the dark brown bear let out a ghastly gnashing roar. Lars and Mats seemingly flew back across the stream, howling in fear. The bear's eyes followed them.

Emil had drawn his knife and yelled, "No, no, don't run! Only food runs!" There were no trees close enough to save them. Cloud looked at Emil, then the bear, and charged into the stream, baring his teeth in a fierce wolf snarl.

Kilan frantically jumped splashing into the river. The Grizzly followed with a snort, catching him midstream. A huge paw smashed the struggling boy into the water, pinning him there. A barking Cloud splashing toward him was his last sensation, then there was nothing but blackness. Kilan never heard the sudden whistling sound. A thin wooden blur thumped into the bear's dusty shoulder with great force.

Bret's venom dart had caught the nut-brown Grizzly just behind the shoulder. The bruin bellowed in pain then grunted harshly, snapping savagely at the dart. It left the prone boy and powered forward across the stream. The Grizzly grumbled toward the cool little hunter with a deep, frothy rage. Bret gave ground slowly but surely. With Cloud harassing the enraged splashing bear, he couldn't risk another dart from this angle. The bruin facing two threats halted in indecision. The white wolf was striking at him from one side. It wheeled back suddenly at the white wolf with lightning speed. Cloud barely ducked under a mighty crippling paw stroke. Massive Grizzly jaws snapped shut with a crunch, barely a hair's breadth behind the rolling wolf. Cloud was too fast.

The great bear glared at Bret once again, surging forward with irresistible force as the white wolf nipped at his heels. Then the

Grizzly began wobbling a bit. Bret made ready to thrust with his spear and drew his obsidian knife.

Another whistling dart from the other side slammed the bear in the neck. The bear's spine-chilling roars became a marbled gurgle. The Grizzly finally dropped to its knees. The venom was taking effect.

Papa splashed over to Kilan while Bret quickly finished the bear with his spear. Papa saw the unconscious boy was scratched up with a broken arm. *He's breathing strong. No other visible damage.* Cloud was now growling up beyond the hill, and bear woofs and barks could be heard from that direction.

Papa threw Kilan over his shoulder and hoarsely gasped, "Boys, we are leaving. Bret take point, I'll follow behind."

The little hunter smoothly reloaded his throwing stick and led the way. The boys were still standing there shaking in their shock.

Papa now boomed in the command voice he'd used with his hunting team, "BOYS, move. Drop the fish. FOLLOW BRET. MOVE NOW!" Emil had never heard Papa raise his voice before.

The three boys snapped to attention as if woken from a sleepy trance. They quickly followed Bret and Cloud away from the river. Papa turned to look back. *There's rustling movement in the bushes coming down the hill. There are bears all over reacting to the noise. This is bad.*

Papa lumbered on as fast as possible, following the boys up over a small rise. He glanced back repeatedly to make sure they weren't being stalked. There was bear sign everywhere and they could all hear bear woofs and see birds flying out of bushes to either side. Bret led them across a rocky meadow and onto the main trail. He was waiting there with the boys when Papa caught up.

"Why are we stopping?" whispered a breathless Papa. There was a huge bear scat below him.

Bret knelt, pointing to the trail. "We have fresh bear tracks and scat here and ahead of us all over this trail. The wind is behind us. There are huge sections of berry bushes as far as I can see to either side, which is where I'd be napping if I was a lovesick bear! I don't think Cloud will be able to smell them ahead. How's Kilan?"

Papa muttered, "Maybe the lovesick bears are nicer? Let's not find out. Kilan will have one evil headache when he wakes up. Once the healers set his arm again, he'll be fine. Bret, you are asking me trail or bushes?"

Bret responded by nervously scanning the bushes on either side of the trail again. Cloud snarled again at something back over the hill behind them. Something big and hairy was stalking them.

Papa decided, "We move much faster and see better on the trail—keep Cloud close. Either way, let's clear all these heavy berry bushes fast. Let's move."

Bret grinned darkly. "Good, Aash, did I ever tell you I hate eating fish?'

As absurdly perilous as their situation was, Papa couldn't let this slide. "What do you mean you don't like fish? You are the best fisherman of the People. How is this even possible?

The little hunter's eyes kept scanning for danger. His voice was like someone debating the weather.

"I don't know. Fish don't taste bad, but they don't fill me up. I don't like all the little bones or the scales either. Scales remind me of snakes. I hate snakes. Do you like fish?"

Bret rechecked his venom dart and wordlessly led them down the old game trail. He was gliding ahead with his head on a constant swivel.

Papa realized the little hunter was absorbed in this discussion despite the circumstances. Bret's voice maintained the tone of debating apples versus oranges. The little hunter wasn't crazy—they'd both seen what a Grizzly could do to a man. Aash realized he was in the presence of a truly courageous soul. *We're surrounded by who knows how many Grizzlies! It's one thing to do your duty and learn to control your fear. If Bret cares about death, he certainly didn't show it.*

They pushed hard down the gritty trail at a good pace. Bret was poring over the backwoods trail sign like he was a bear himself. He moved them instinctively to avoid ambush sites.

They were all thirsty, dusty, and breathing hard with dry throats when they finally cleared the berry bush maze. Bret stopped them again on the crest of a pinecone-laden hill. The boys caught their breath in shallow gasps as Papa switched shoulders with Kilan. *The boy's conscious again and asking for his mama.* Papa thought, *This is a good sign.*

The winding game trail narrowed into a singular bushy ridge. There was a concentrated tangle of dark green evergreen trees extending downhill on one side. A large leafy grassy meadow extended uphill on the other. Bret made his way back to Papa, whispering his thoughts.

"Once we pass this ridge, we're back to open flat plains the rest of the way. Visibility is much better here. I think that bear's mate may be what's following us. She's gaining on us. We can't outrun her. You can't fight well carrying the boy. Let's switch. You lead the boys with Cloud. I'll follow in case that broken hearted she-bear doesn't quit."

Papa didn't like it, but Bret was right. The greater danger was likely now following close behind. Papa now led the group forward while the little hunter tested the air behind them for trouble.

There was another throaty roar somewhere behind them. The forest came alive around them with the sounds of frightened birds. Bret's ankle was completely red and swollen now. He gritted forward, silently chanting his war mantra. "Now I am become Death, the destroyer of worlds." The little hunter forced a grin despite his parched throat and the dull throbbing in his ankle. He checked the mounting on his last venom dart to make sure it was sound.

It happened fast. They'd just barely heard the bellows of red deer when a broad rising wave of thrashing hooves and snapping brush exploded up onto the trail. A spooked herd of deer stampeded the trail from the dense tangle below. The air suddenly seemed full of leaping deer any way you looked. Papa dropped to a knee, holding on to Kilan, while the boys instinctively knelt and covered their heads. Panicked deer were flying between, over, and around them. There was a bone-jarring crash behind them and a shocked wheezing groan. A startled stag had crashed right into Bret, with the powerful antlers impaling the little hunter straight through the chest. The frantic buck began stomping him with its sharp hooves, before escaping uphill into the grassy plain with the herd.

Papa checked the boys quickly, and made his way to the little hunter's prone body. Oh no, Bret! The stag's horns had gone clean through the heart. Bret was down and barely making bubbly gurgling sounds. Papa held the dying man in his arms and put his ear down close.

"The boys...?" rasped Bret.

"They're fine, Bret...Bret, stay with me," commanded Papa softly. *No. No. No!*

The little hunter had a peaceful, all-knowing look in his eye. He gurgled out, "I'm sorry, Aash. Give Emil my knife," as the light went out of his eyes. Bret was gone.

The wind switched again and Cloud began growling at something behind them on the trail. Papa gently closed Bret's eyes and scooped up the fallen weapons. He handed Mats the light spear and Emil the black knife.

Papa ordered, "Bret's gone, boys. Now we run for the village. Emil, take Cloud and lead. That Grizzly is still coming. Boys, keep running with Cloud, no matter what you hear behind you. MOVE!" Kilan had passed out again. Aash scooped him up and followed as fast as possible with the heavy spear in one hand and the unconscious boy slung over his shoulder.

The boys and Papa made it over the last hill and were well into the silver-brown savannah when they heard it. The wind carried faint echoes of a wailing brown Grizzly in the hills behind them. Papa kept switching shoulders and checking behind them, but the bear wasn't coming anymore.

The weary band hobbled back to the village without further ado, in an amber hue, as the lazy failing sun gave way to rapidly rising dusk.

Chapter Fifteen
Good

"God is good, but never dance with a lion."
-Zimbabwean Proverb

THE WEARY MUD-CAKED LITTLE boys collapsed into a crying huddle upon finally reaching the village. Their grateful mothers scooped them all up with tight tearful hugs while their fathers were unsuccessfully trying to look stern.

Mama and Papa hugged with touching heads and a sobbing Emil carried between them. Emil was inconsolable. "I knew it was a mistake. I made the second mistake, Mama. The second mistake, and Bret's gone just like Dori."

Papa softly told Emil it wasn't true but let him get the tears out. Mama took Emil and Cloud back to the Gher. Chief Sev had also wanted to say something stern to the boys but thought better after hearing Emil's weeping words. *Life is hard for the*

People, he reminded himself. *The boys went for fish to help feed the People. They'd been foolish but brave.*

Papa talked the noticeably silent Chief through the day's events. Chief Sev suddenly punched his palm, glaring up at the Sky Spirits.

"Bret, little Bret. Our best hunter. Bret survives a suicide mission over the river. He kills the Sabretooth single-handed, as well as a Grizzly. Then he's accidentally killed by a panicked deer? I should have ordered him to stay in his Gher for three full days after the Sabretooth. How many deer has Bret taken with that light spear over the seasons? How is any of this possible, Aash?"

The Chief lashed out, kicking a protruding piece of kindling from the nearest fire. Sparks flashed out in the darkness like a swarm of fireflies. He looked around. No one else had seen this outburst. Chief Sev quickly regained his composure. *It's always the heroes we lose...*

Papa cleared his throat and took a deep breath to steady his voice.

"Bret was the reason we made it back. I think the bear's mate was stalking us the whole way and she spooked the deer. Nothing else makes sense. We need to bring Bret home."

"I'll lead a team to get him at first light," swore the Chief. "Get some rest, Spearmaker."

Emil and Mama were already asleep, exhausted from the day when Papa got to the Gher. None of them had any appetite.

Cloud came over and licked Papa's hand. He scratched the white wolf behind the ears and gave him a choice cut of meat from the evening meal. Cloud had been a big part of their survival today as well. The wolf smell had kept the vengeful she-bear cautious and back.

The next morning Stygian darkness gave way to a glowing red sunrise. Tomorrow comes like it always does, no matter what good or bad has happened today. The air had a crisp frost and the birds were again flying very low. Emil sat in Mama's lap sipping some water. The morning was telling them a storm was coming.

"Mama, I knew we shouldn't go. If I had said more, we wouldn't have gone. Now Bret is dead," whispered Emil.

Mama's blue eyes looked softly at her son as she raised his chin up. She instructed in a strong but gentle voice:

"Bret would be the first to tell you the Eagle Feather was the greatest hunter of the People. Did you know your opa was too anxious to see a bison hunt as a boy? He actually watched from under a cliff as the hunters stampeded the herd off of it. Somehow, he escaped unharmed, but several boys who followed him were hurt or killed. This makes sense when you are standing under a cliff raining bison. He learned his lesson and never did anything so foolish again.

"The same happened to me too. When I first started helping gather fruits, I once saw a beautiful tree with graceful flowing leaves and little red berries. I picked a basket full and they were mixed up with other fruits we had picked. They were yew berries. The fruit is edible but the seeds and leaves are very poisonous. If an Elder hadn't noticed before the evening meal that day, many of us would have died. Your papa too. He nearly burned half the village down. As a boy Papa once accidentally set fire to the Elder's Gher when he tripped with a torch. Just once though."

Mama sang Babo's favorite songs with him that morning, comforting him like only a mother can. Papa watched quietly, thinking, *There is something magical about when a woman becomes a mother.*

Emil was still silent after morning chores, quietly cuddled again in Mama's lap, and listening to Papa.

"Babo, life is hard, we make mistakes, we learn from them. It was good you told Shala or we'd never have known. If Bret knew how things would turn out, he'd still have gone. That's who he was. Let's both earn the gift he gave us. Earn it, Emil."

Chief Sev and the hunting team were back before midday. They brought back the little hunter's throwing stick; otherwise there was nothing left of Bret's body. The bear had eaten all of it and there were signs it was still in the area. Deep, angry claw marks were carved into every nearby tree.

The Spirit Ceremony for Bret was short and to the point, just as he would have wanted. Chief Sev was deeply emotional.

"My people, death smiles at us all. We can only smile back. It was a good death, a warrior's death. Bret died saving little ones, something any warrior would be proud of."

The Chief then tried to imitate Bret's turtle dance. This folly, though unsuccessful, still brought a wistful smile to every tearful face.

Life was hard for the People. Kilan's arm was hanging in a deerskin sling and his scratches were laced with healing herbal paste. The boy sincerely thanked Papa and gave Cloud a big piece of meat and a hug.

Papa could see still the guilt in all the little boys' eyes. He told Mama he'd take them out to pick some winter berries before the storm.

The boys busily plucked the ruby red little berries, but were too quiet. Papa suddenly began howling like a wolf and throwing berries at the boys and Cloud. There was a full-on howling, berry-throwing food fight in progress. The shrieking boys began ducking and weaving, and pelting Papa with the little red berries. Faint smiles briefly appeared on resilient young faces.

Papa sat the boys in a circle, asking, "What made Bret a great hunter? He wasn't the biggest or strongest; for a long time the People made fun of him. I think it was the word good."

The boys all looked puzzled. *The word good?*

Papa went on and explained.

"Bret was a little hunter with the strongest spirit of the People. Whenever something went wrong, his only response was always 'good.' They said he was too small to be on a hunting team. Bret just said, 'Good.' Then he worked with the Eagle Feather to track better than anyone. One man, especially a smaller man, is always quieter in the woods than four. They said he couldn't have a heavy spear. Bret said 'good,' then become a master with the light spear. They said he was too small to hunt big game. Bret just said 'good' and became a master fisherman. The People's smallest hunter still developed the skill to kill a Sabretooth alone. Boys, you can learn everything a man needs from Bret's spirit. He was wise enough to know himself. Bret was sharp enough to focus on his strengths. His hunting style emphasized speed and silence, which are much easier for a smaller man. Whenever something goes wrong, just say 'good' and 'better' yourself. This is the ancient way of warriors and hunters. We just say 'good,' adapt, improvise, and overcome."

The boys began murmuring "good" to themselves.

A berry-splattered Papa said, "All right hunters, storm coming. Back home we go!"

The boys were still a bit quiet, but chattering again. Cloud was barking up a storm, hopping around chasing squirrels up trees.

Emil took Papa's hand in his as they walked. "Good, at least we won't have to eat as much silvery bony fish now," he said in a brave little voice.

Papa chuckled. "Good, yes, and I won't have to make those pesky little light spears anymore."

Emil ran his hand over the black knife in its flying fish sheath and looked up at Papa. Both of their eyes were misty. Papa put a proud hand on his son's shoulder for the rest of the walk back to the village.

As the boys neared the village, they joked and chased Cloud and one another. The sun was at its zenith for the day. The boys still had to hunt eggs and fetch wood for the day. They all hurriedly dropped off their berries and grabbed their egg pouches.

They passed Bret's Gher when Papa asked about the little hunter's spear. Emil opened the flap to retrieve it. He coughed as dense, hazy blue smoke filled the inside of the Gher completely. In his exhaustion Emil had left the spear standing inside with a single fish from his pouch. He had forgotten to open the Gher's smoke hole at the top last night. They had to wait for enough fresh air to go inside.

Cloud was eyeing this fish hungrily. Papa saw the fish had a different darker color and a new smokey smell. *This is odd. The fish has a distinct woody smell, but it's not spoiled.*

Papa was still going to throw it out when they reached their Gher. *Cloud really wants to eat it.* Mama noticed this, sniffed it, and tried a little bite. The fish tasted different but not bad and surprisingly wasn't spoiled. Many nights later the fish still was dry to the taste, but not spoiled. Somehow the heavy smoke from the closed Gher had cured the fish overnight.

Over the next cycle of the moon, Mama and Emil practiced smoking small strips of daily game in Bret's Gher. The fish lasted several days. The meat, especially venison, lasted for even longer.

A cycle of the moon later, snow covered the ground. The village faced a food shortage as they did with every winter. There were no fruits or eggs, and hunting large animals in heavy snow was difficult.

Papa invited the Chief and the elders to Bret's Gher. Mama offered them all strips of smoked venison. The Elders cautiously sniffed the strange smoky smell. Papa and Emil ate their strips and drank some water. Chief Sev bit his strip, observing, "This is deer but tastes different. Where did you get this?"

"This comes from the last deer we caught after the Spirit Ceremony," said Papa.

Sev's wide-eyed response was, "That was a full moon cycle ago, even before the snows. How is this possible?"

Papa took a long sip of water then replied, "Emil forgot a fish in this Gher with the fire still going and the smoke hole closed. We found the fish was changed but still edible several days later. It was some power of the smoke. We've been smoking a bit of the daily game for the last moon cycle."

Chief Sev thought deeply. His eyes smiled back and forth between Emil and the venison. He looked the boy in the eye. *This smoked meat could change everything for us.*

"Do you realize this means we can take more game in times of plenty and store it for moon cycles? Smoked game taken in the fall can help us get through the winter. Now our hunting teams and the whole village can move further and longer. It means we can avoid wars over hunting grounds. We can keep meat without hunting for some time if need be."

Chief Sev was truly astonished. He addressed the group again.

"Life is such a mystery. If the Eagle Feather hadn't vouched for him, little Bret would never have been trained as a hunter. Think of his effect on the People. Where would we be without his skill with the Mountain Men and the Sabretooth? Then you two save the boys. In a way, because of Bret and Emil, now we've learned to smoke meat. One good decision can impact so much."

Chapter Sixteen
Mountain Woman

"Kindness can pluck the whiskers of a lion."
-Moroccan Proverb

AN EARLY MORNING TWILIGHT illuminated the frosty north wind as she kissed icy sleet across the forest. The powerful arctic winds had frozen the Mountain River solid.

Cloud and Papa plodded a rough trail through the snow. Emil and the village boys followed single file. They were hurrying to pick snow oranges from the icy gnarled groves by the river. A foreboding winter storm wasn't far over the horizon. There wasn't a single animal in sight. It seemed the entire forest knew this.

Papa was sweating from the exertion of breaking a snow trail despite the sharp chill in the air. He drank from his water pouch, reminding the boys to do the same.

"The cold can make you forget thirst," he reminded, as he stopped just ahead of the orange tree copse. "Snow is good for tracking, but harder for us to move through. See how much easier it is for Cloud. This is why wolves rule the winter. Look at the broad pads on Cloud's paws."

Papa pointed his heavy spear at the nearest orange tree. "Pick the fruit fast, then we'll look at the ice river. Form pairs and watch out for sinkholes."

Emil had learned sinkholes could be dangerous in snow country, especially if you are alone. The branches of snow-covered trees could create a treacherous hollow around the trunk. This pit could trap and kill you.

Papa next led them to the ice river. He showed the boys the difference between smooth ice and jagged ice. The latter often has dangerous running water under it. Papa told them to walk across frozen water with your arms held out sideways, or with a spear held horizontally in front of you. You have a chance to stop your fall if the ice cracks under you. It's even safer to crawl on ice.

Cloud was slipping on the ice cracks and yapping at a sizeable jagged hole near the middle of the river. Papa left the boys ashore and cautiously crawled out to Cloud. There were two sets of tracks. One was a small person who had been running across the ice. The second set of tracks looked like moose, but ended at the broken ice hole. The sign told Papa a small Mountain Man had been chased across the frozen river by a big moose. The ice had cracked under the creature's weight and the moose was gone. Papa and Cloud followed the tracks back to the People's side of the river. Once in the snow, Papa read the tracks. *It's either a small woman or a child.*

Papa called the boys over close to him. Cloud sniffed the footprints and they followed him. The tracks led back in the direction of the village. Cloud led them to a small tangle of trees. Papa could see a berry pouch and a furry boot sticking out of a shallow snowbank. Papa and the boys dug out a small mountain woman. She was unconscious and slightly frostbitten, but still barely breathing. There was dried rust-colored snow and a jagged bone protruding from her lower leg.

Emil asked, "Aren't we going to help her, Papa, she's hurt?"

Aash paused and looked at his son. *It should be that simple, but it isn't. This woman is a trespasser from a hostile tribe on our territory.* A member of the People on the other side of the river should expect to be killed in a similar situation. There were too many dark acts on both sides in the last war. Aash had every right to kill her, but knew he couldn't.

If the Mountain Men come looking for her or if they think the People have taken her, it could be war. It might be easier just to leave her, though. This is the safest option. She's not our responsibility and could lead to war.

While Papa mulled these risks over, the boys had meanwhile made their choice. They propped her up. Her pulse was strong and Cloud was licking her face. All the little boys were now staring up expectantly at him. Papa shrugged and threw her over his shoulder. *The boys are right, we'll try to save her.*

The village was all stares when this motley crew arrived. Papa handed her off to Mama and a gaggle of startled women from the village. Mama helped carry her into a warm Gher.

Chief Sev recognized the furs of the Mountain People, asking, "Exactly what is going on here, Spearmaker?"

Papa's reply was low and soft. "We found her by the ice river. Moose attack. We couldn't leave her." He cut the Chief's reply off. "I know, I know, I know."

The Elder Healer reported from the Gher after the evening meal. "The Mountain Woman is very weak. Her leg is broken. She probably won't survive the night. We'll warm her and see."

Chief Sev just stared silently at Papa. *The bloody Mountain Man War could happen again.*

Mama helped the healers with the Mountain Woman. They set her broken leg and warmed her under sleeping furs. She was murmuring in her sleep in the Mountain language. Mama recognized the word "Moose." The woman had a beautiful ivory necklace which she kept yanking in her sleep. Mama was scared she might break it in her tossing fits. Lulu carefully removed it and wrapped it in a small fur hide to the side. Mama noticed there were no forest sounds that night as she made her way back to their Gher. The nocturnal winds were picking up swirling force. She could see the village Gher bindings swaying back and forth in the gale.

Emil was cuddled with Cloud and blissfully snoring away as Mama entered the Gher. Papa had a pensive look on his face. He warmed into a smile when he saw her.

"I think she makes it," opined Mama as she climbed into the sleeping furs.

"We did the right thing. This could still go bad," worried Papa.

Mama's voice was tired but even.

"We've not had war with the Mountain Men since I was a child. This poor woman also endured the Sabretooth. She's never harmed the People. She was just picking berries when attacked by a moose. She is someone's daughter, sister, mother, wife, or all of these things. I'm proud we are helping her. It tells me we are living the things we teach Babo. Maybe she'll be well enough to return to her tribe in a few days."

"Yes," answered Papa as he held her close. *That moose could just as easily have attacked one of us. If it was you, my love, I'd come no matter where the tracks led. Her husband will come. Their warriors may all come soon. That's the risk.*

Mama, as always, could read his silent thoughts and smiled appreciatively. *Yes, nothing would stop you.*

She brushed the soft spot on his forehead. "Maybe we send a team to watch the river and sign to the Mountain Men we saved her. Perhaps take her hat as proof?"

They both watched Emil and Cloud cuddled up and smiled, realizing the two were snoring in unison. Papa liked her plan and decided to share it with Chief Sev at dawn.

The polar graying light of a fresh winter morning filtered into focus. Chief Sev was bundled up in a fur robe and smoking a long black pipe. He listened to the Spearmaker in silence.

The Chief finally spoke, "Good, Spearmaker. The Mountain Woman's fever has broken but she's still weak. You lead a team out there immediately. I want someone calm in charge."

The arctic wind suddenly snapped a taut leather Gher binding rope. It sent a rock sailing into the trees. Papa gave Mama and Babo kisses just before leaving. Emil stared at the forest and said, "Cloud, go with Papa."

As it turned out, it was very good Emil did this. The crimson sky and low-flying birds told them to hurry.

Aash was thrilled to be breathing the crisp winter air and leading a hunting team again. Even if only for a single day. Cloud briskly led them to the ice river in the area of the Mountain Woman's tracks. Aash stayed with Cloud while splitting the team into pairs. They spread out across the riverbank. In this way, they could cover and watch a greater area of the ice river for the Mountain Men. The team knew to call out and come together at contact. Aash and the hunters climbed slippery trees. They watched and waited as the glistening frozen ice shimmered in front of them. Then the tired sun was being roughly cast out of the sky by swiftly flowing dark clouds. The white wolf napped at the base of Aash's tree.

In the healers' Gher, Mama was wringing out a wet poultice from the Mountain Woman's head. The Elder Healer palmed the woman's head, saying, "The fever is gone, she'll wake up soon."

The Elder turned for a new poultice. The Mountain Woman sat up quickly, snatching up a nearby skinning blade. She grabbed the Elder by the hair and pulled her close while painfully sliding back to the wall of the Gher. She held the knife to the healer's throat, while screeching unintelligible words in an unmistakably menacing tone.

Mama drew her black knife and looked the Mountain Woman straight in the eye. Lulu made the peace sign. The Mountain Woman repeated her harsh words and yanked on the Elder's hair.

Mama pointed to herself and smiled. She voiced softly, "Lulu, Lulu, I am Lulu, we won't hurt you." She could see the primal fear in the Mountain Woman's fiery eyes.

Mama had an idea. She took a slow step back and pointed to the fur that held the ivory necklace, then slowly reached for it. She showed the woman her ivory necklace and placed it within easy reach. Then Mama signed. "Moose attack…my man finds you…we fix leg," and pointed at the broken leg.

The Mountain Woman hesitated and stopped her harsh words. She peeked under the sleeping furs and saw the fresh poultice on her leg. She sniffed the healing herbs from the poultice.

Mama reached for a water pouch, took a quick sip, and offered it to the Mountain Woman. The parched woman picked it up slowly. She sniffed it and took a quick cautious sip.

Mama took another chance. *I need to calm her down.* She put her black knife down where she could still reach it, then signed again, "Lulu, Lulu, Lulu."

The Mountain Woman's fiery green eyes met Mama's placid blue ones. She released the Elder, who scrambled behind Lulu. The little woman kept the knife close but pointed at herself. "Inga, I am Inga," she signed. Then she put down the knife and put on her ivory necklace.

Mama signed, "We take...you back...to your people." And offered her some meat.

The Mountain Woman took a big bite of salty meat and chewed ravenously. She looked at the tall blue-eyed woman across the Gher and signed. "My man crazy...he come for me."

Lulu grinned knowingly. "My man crazy too...I lost...he do...same."

The women both smiled at this. Then Inga grimaced at the pain from her leg. Before long they had signed to each other how many children each had and shared their names. Ironically, in just the short amount of time it took the women to find peace, their men were on the cusp of war.

The Mountain Men came in a full hunting team. They were fierce, bearded giants. Aash took in their ivory war axes and watched their bearing and spacing. The smallest man was their leader, and still a full head taller than any of the People. The Mountain Men halted halfway across the river at the moose hole. One of them was a truly massive red-bearded man.

These men are experienced and disciplined warriors, thought Aash. *The red-bearded giant looks as ferocious as a Grizzly himself in his furs.*

Aash's team had loaded their throwing sticks, but kept them pointed at the ground. They walked slowly onto the ice river, calling out so the Mountain Men could see them. Aash stopped and held out his heavy spear horizontally in front of him in the peace sign. The leader of the Mountain Men did the same. They would parley.

Aash told his team to be ready but stay put for now. He'd reminded them the Mountain Men fight with two axes, one of which they throw. Aash walked out to meet the Mountain Men with Cloud.

He could see curious looks on the opposing faces, as they took in his throwing stick and solo approach. They mostly saw a fierce white wolf silently gliding with him like a deadly ghost over the ice. *Cloud clearly unsettles these giants. Good.*

There was something else. What Aash didn't know was the legend of Fenrir. The Mountain Men believed a great wolf named Fenrir was trapped by the Sky Spirits in the heavens.

When this wolf finally gnawed his way free, the world would end. The man approaching them commanded a powerful wolf. They all thought of the legend.

At a twenty-pace distance Aash halted across from the four bearded giants. "I am Aash, son of the Eagle Feather...," he signed, "why you come...our lands?"

By their reaction, it was clear they knew of the Eagle Feather. Their leader signed back, "I am Vili, son of Damon...the river is not your lands...we look for woman."

Aash nodded and pointed at the ice hole. "Moose attack woman.... we save her," he signed.

At this the massive red-bearded man let out a sigh of relief.

Aash signed to him. "Your woman?"

The Redbeard nodded, pointing to himself. "Aki."

Aash signed, "Her leg broken...we bring here...in morning."

The Redbeard signed harshly, "No, bring now!"

Aash pointed at the red sky, signing, "Big, big storm coming. We bring after.... she weak."

The Redbeard took a menacing step forward, as did Cloud, before their leader also pointed to the sky and snapped something at him. Vili turned back to Aash and signed, "You come with us...until after storm." Aash didn't trust this man. *There's something cruel in his eyes.*

Three things then happened simultaneously. First, Cloud sensed their tone and began a deep menacing growl while stepping protectively in front of Aash. The Mountain Men all shifted forward with their axes ready. Aash raised his throwing stick. The obsidian point of his venom dart gleamed in the final fleeting sunlight. "No," he said in a firm low voice. Aash's hunting team quickly came up to defend him with throwing sticks ready. The ice river was deathly quiet now.

The Mountain Men paused. They had never seen a wolf do this. *This was great magic.*

Aash looked their leader in the eye, signing, "We bring her after storm...or we all die here."

Then he reassured Redbeard, signing, "Aki...I bring your woman after storm...No war."

Aash looked at Vili.

I don't like this. The little Mountain Man isn't convinced. Aki's the biggest threat. He gets the venom dart. Cloud might delay them enough to reload. No, too close after the dart, it'll be heavy spear versus axe.

Vili assessed the command presence of the quiet man facing him. In the end, it came down to the dark brown eyes calmly assessing him.

This man controls a white wolf and carries the scars of countless hunts on his body. The Eagle Feather was an unholy terror in the last war. He'd killed our chief in single combat. This one, his son, would see something through to the end.

Vili signed, taunting with a black-hearted grin. "Son of the Eagle Feather...I thought you would be taller."

Aash's lipless, wolfish smile whispered, "Me too." He kept his eyes focused on Vili as he subtly shifted his weight toward Aki for the coming throw.

A clap of thunder rumbled in the heavens, shaking all of them like rats. All of them except for Cloud. Everyone noticed the white wolf hadn't even blinked and was staring at Vili's throat with chilling blue-eyed ferocity. The great winter storm announced itself without warning. Rude, hard hail crashed everywhere as the howling sky rapidly darkened with wild winds. The greatest danger now for all was the storm. This would be a severe blizzard. Everyone had to get off the ice.

"Bring woman here after storm," signed Vili. He turned abruptly back for their shore, and the Mountain Men followed suit. The Redbeard hesitated until Aash reassured him with a final nod.

Cloud rapidly led Aash and the hunting team back to the village. Visibility vanished into whiteout. *We may have stayed too late. Cloud will get us home.* Aash huddled the team and had them tie themselves together. The blizzard screeched wildly with gale force winds. They eventually returned safely despite the conditions due to Cloud. Aash realized Emil sending Cloud had likely saved him twice that day.

The ice blizzard lasted through the night and finally broke near the following dusk. A fresh blanket of deep, powdery, sparkling snow encompassed the landscape as far as the eye could see. The birds were all back, vigorously chirping again, as the fleeting purple sunlight briefly reappeared as well.

Inga the Mountain Woman had recovered a great deal. She sat with the women by the fires. The fierce little woman was excited to learn she would be returned at dawn. Inga eagerly insisted on helping cook the evening meal. Her sable furs were much warmer than any in the village. She was the only woman not shivering by the evening fires.

The village women joked as the meat sizzled. Inga had taken this opportunity to braid Lulu's hair in the style of the Mountain Women. This feat was of no small interest to the People's women, who circled up close. Lulu was always beautiful to Aash, but especially today. Papa noted the two of them were giggling like long-lost sisters.

Inga saw Mama salting the steaming meat, and asked what this was. After one piece she declared salted meat tasted so much better. She noticed Mama shivering a bit at a wind gust. Inga put her warm sable hat on Lulu's head. The two women somehow figured out only the People's lands had salt licks. Sable were much more common in the mountains of Inga's people.

At the evening meal the children were fed first. Inga was sitting next to Mama and Emil. She handed the boy a sizzling piece of salted meat on a big leaf. There was a faded jagged scar on her hand which Emil asked about.

The Mountain Woman signed, "Skorpon," and made a biting motion. Mama and all of the village women stopped serving and stared at her. The Skorpon was a small red insect with cruel pincers and a barbed sharp tail. Its sting was deadly. There was no cure and anyone stung died a painful death within a day. Mama signed to Inga "Skorpon" and made the death sign.

Inga shook her head. She stopped eating to reach for her small fur pouch. She pulled out a tiny dried white flower, saying, "Edelweiss."

The Mountain Woman rubbed the dried white flower over the bite scar and signed to the group, "Skorpon...Edelweiss. Skorpon bite bad...Edelweiss save good."

Mama took the white flower in her hand. This was a mountain flower that didn't grow in the People's lands. Inga took the edelweiss back in her hand and held up one finger. She rubbed the flower into her scar again. Then she held up a second finger and acted as if she was adding the flower to her water pouch and drinking it. Then she smiled at all of them.

That night Inga sang along with the People at the evening meal. She really wanted to dance along with the women, but her leg was still healing. Mama put an arm around her and held Inga up. The two danced a hop on three legs. Mama saw Papa clapping in approval.

"Do you like my hair this way?" Lulu asked.

Aash replied, "That's a silly question. I'm the wrong person to ask. You know you're always the most beautiful thing in the world to me. Hair or no hair. Snow or sun. Since the first moment I saw you. Yes, I do like it this new way too."

Then it was time for the men to dance. Emil and the boys wanted to dance with the men, so they did. The boys jumped as high as they could for courage, just like their fathers. Emil tried Bret's turtle dance, and almost pulled it off. It was one of those warm, cozy winter nights you never want to end.

The Mountain Woman was returned to her people the next morning on a fur-lined travois. In addition, Inga was returned with two large leather pouches of salt. The Mountain Man team was once again led by Vili, whose serpentine eyes remained glacial.

Aki the red-bearded giant glided gracefully across the ice and scooped up Inga with glee. Aash nodded to Vili and the couple, and turned back for shore with Cloud.

"Aash," called out Aki. He signed," My woman...tell...you find...save her."

Aash turned and signed, "Yes."

Aki signed, "When war comes, I kill you last." But his smile said he was joking. This crack earned him a quick slap from his fierce little wife. The giant laughed heartily again and put Inga down gingerly. Aki did not believe in the legend of Fenrir, but he still kept a cautious eye on Cloud. Aash had not missed this, or how light on his feet this powerful giant moved. *It's hard not to like this merry mountain of a man.*

The red-bearded giant stood tall and signed again. "Son of Eagle Feather, your spear is too short." Aki swept the frost from his bright red beard. Aash's hunting team raised their spears.

Aash signed back, "Not if you dance close enough," while taking a smiling step forward.

The bear-sized man's rolling laugh echoed again across the sparkling ice river. He picked up his great ivory war axe, twirling the heavy hatchet deftly in a meaty paw as if were a twig. Aki very slowly offered it handle side forward to Aash. "A real weapon...you take...Son of Eagle Feather."

Aash graciously accepted the gift. Inga called him over as well and held out her ivory necklace.

"Give Lulu," she signed. "In one moon cycle...my man...bring sable furs...you bring salt."

Once again Aash caught the momentary look of malice on Vili's face. *Some men just want to see the world burn, thought Aash. If there is war with the Mountain Men, it'll be due to him.*

As Cloud led the way home, Aash was deep in thought.

These Mountain Men are huge with pale skin, but otherwise so similar to the People. They also love one another and struggle to survive, just like us. There might still be war over land or game. I know now the Mountain Men aren't just the barbaric savages of the stories.

Aash had been raised to believe there are only the People, enemies, and strangers who must be considered enemies.

Does it have to be this way? He thought of fighting mighty Aki. The jolly giant had been one step away from learning the true power of a "little" venom dart. *This thought is surprisingly bothersome. Mighty Aki reminds me of little Bret in jaunty spirit.*

There are also women like Inga, who'd have fit right in with the People's women.

Aash looked at the glistening ivory war axe. He marveled at the folly of twirling it.

It's a magnificent weapon. It would take me two hands just to wield it. Trading salt for furs is a good start, and a much better use of our hands than war. The Mountain Men can be reasoned with.

Chapter Seventeen
Snow

"The whisper of a pretty girl can be heard further off than the roar of a lion."
-French Proverb

A GHASTLY, YET MELODIOUS sound rang throughout the stark star-kissed darkness of the winter sky. The village Ghers swayed heavily in the frosty nocturnal winds. Cloud's ears had perked up at the haunting howls of the wolves. The white wolf and Emil looked at each other, then howled back in reply. The entire Gher was filled with howls as Mama and Papa joined them. *We are a pack, a family, life is good.*

"Will they come, Papa?" Emil asked.

Papa went back to whittling a knife handle. "When they come, wolves are a silent wind rustling over a single pinecone. They tolerate and avoid us for the most part. When they howl it's to find each other, mark territory, and maybe because just like us, they like to sing."

Mama and Emil went back to playing Eagle Eye. Babo was getting almost as good as Mama.

"What is territory?" asked the boy.

Mama answered, "It's an area or land that animals or people feel they own. They live there, eat there, and will fight for it."

Emil was confused and tapped his finger on his cheek.

Mama went on, "Think of a tiger. It lives in a certain part of the forest and stays within this beat. It hunts for food here and marks its area by roaring, clawing trees, or scent marks. They are warning other tigers to stay away from their food. Most animals prefer to avoid us. If you get too close, they turn and fight just like we would."

Emil blurted out, "This is why we stay on this side of the river, and the Mountain Men on the other side. Will we ever have to fight them again? They are so big."

Papa looked at Mama's ivory necklace. Her blonde locks were still braided in the new style of the Mountain Women. "I don't think so, Babo. It was good we saved Inga and now we trade salt for furs. No one wants war. There is enough game on both sides of the river, and plenty of water for all. You are right, they are big and powerful. The war with them was very bad for the People."

"How did we win? It's because we were smarter." stated Emil.

Papa shook his head, and picked up the Mountain Man's heavy ivory war axe. The weapon was perfectly balanced for throwing.

"No, they are smart too. In the end it was a very close thing. Some of it was luck, but mainly we made them fight our fight. We learned real fast facing them in the open with their size and these big throwing axes was bad. They are so much bigger and stronger than us. Your opa adapted our strategy to our strengths. We are faster and much better in the woods. We would ambush them in the woods and melt away too fast for them. We'd set traps for them in the forest and raid them at night, which no one does. They'd taunt us to come out in the open and fight like men. That's nonsense—if you have to fight, fight to win. Fight to your strengths if possible. They'd track us and lose men to traps on the trail. The trail would end in emptiness with nothing there but a single white eagle feather. Then we would ambush them on the way home. We only fought when we had advantage, or they couldn't find us."

Papa paused to look over at Mama.

"We also won because our women were magnificent. They also fought. They were so skilled at breaking down Ghers, moving the village, and keeping us fed. We moved the village so fast and often, the Mountain Men never found us. All our men could fight instead of hunting. We adapt. If we fought again, they would expect such things. With enough throwing sticks and wolves, we could now even face them in the open if needed."

Emil was watching Papa intently, taking all of this in. "What kinds of traps, Papa?"

"Bad ones, Babo," recalled Papa. "We'd leave small hidden pits with sharp stakes where they walked. Sometimes we left a deadly snake staked to a tree branch when they were following us. The angry viper would strike the next person that passed. War is slaughter, Emil."

"Enough war talk, I don't like it," Mama said.

Papa smiled mischievously. "She is right. Playing to your strengths works anywhere. Who is the best runner, wrestler, and thrower among the boys? What if there was a contest with a new light spear as a prize?"

Emil's eyes thought about it. "Mats runs the fastest. Kilan always wins at wrestling, and I throw the best."

Papa grinned. "So in the contest you would each win at what you do best. To win the tiebreaker you would have to wrestle better than Mats, or outrun Kilan. You are the second fastest runner. So, your training focus should be throwing and running before the contest. Do you follow?"

Papa added, "With advantage make the game as simple as possible; if not, make it as complex."

Mama rolled her eyes with nostalgia at this. She shook her head slowly in mock disdain of Papa, and playfully took Emil in her lap.

"Babo, your papa wasn't the strongest or fastest boy in the village. He never won at wrestling, or spear contests. or the Autumn Races. Aron was the fastest boy. Your papa challenged him to a race. He lost the first twenty-nine races, then finally won the thirtieth one. Everyone saw this. He isn't as funny as he thinks he is, and doesn't have a great singing voice either. Naturally, this never stopped him from climbing the tree closest to where the girls sorted the daily fruit and singing to me. Of course, he promptly fell out of the tree and broke his arm. It was pretty obvious he would never be a great hunter or chief. The smart girls were pretty sure he was too clumsy to even survive ten winters. But none of the other boys climbed trees and sang. He only sang to me; he made me laugh!"

"All's fair in love and war," laughed Papa as he gave them both a big kiss.

These old stories always made Emil smile, but there was something else on his mind after hearing the wolves. His mind was flooded with thoughts. He visualized some of the things they'd seen the past few days. Emil especially wondered about some of the pictures on the walls of the Sabretooth's cave.

Papa said these men had powerful spirits that helped them hunt mammoth and other big game. Some of the pictures showed the ancient men had big feet when hunting in winter. Emil also thought about the power of the recent winter storm. *The rough white hail falling from the dark sky had stung harder than thrown rocks. There was so much force to things that fell far.*

Mama and Papa had fallen asleep, as had Cloud. The white wolf was cuddled next to Emil and snoring away. The great gray wolves so far away had stopped serenading the moon that night. Emil fell asleep dreaming of snow, wolves, and mammoths.

The next day was sunny but cold. After morning chores, Papa and the boys were practicing throwing. They could all see their breath. Cloud went off chasing something in the woods.

Papa had set up a target and was practicing with the new ivory axe. It was balanced but heavy and he needed his whole body and both hands to throw it. The boys were throwing light spears and learning to adjust for the wind.

Emil had stopped throwing and was standing in one of Cloud's footprints. Then it came to him.

"Papa, I have an idea. Cloud's heavier than me, but I sink more in the snow. Is it because his feet are bigger or the shape? I think it's the shape because the Mountain Men have really big feet, and they sink even farther. The men in the cave pictures had feet shaped like this."

Emil drew a big oval shape in the snow around his foot then went on, "No people have feet like this. I think they are wearing something this shape on their feet to walk in the snow."

Papa stroked his chin pensively. "It would have to be strong enough to run on though. Wood, I think, with leather straps to hold them on."

They went to the woodpile and Papa found two good broad pieces of wood. He carefully carved out matching teardrop-shaped blades. The next step was adding holes on each side for bindings to pass through. The sun was at its peak for the day, when he called Emil over. Papa had him stand on the blades and secured them tight by tying leather bindings over the feet.

Emil could run over the snow now just like Cloud. The boys each wanted a pair now too. Papa had them test the "snow feet" in deeper powdery snow. It was still much better than before.

Chief Sev had heard the animated boys and came over to watch. He took one blade from Emil and looked it up and down. "This changes winter hunting. All of the People must have them."

Half a moon cycle later, one of the People's hunting teams left at dawn all wearing the "snow feet" and returned at dusk with a massive elk. They had stalked and chased it down through heavy powder wearing the new wooden feet. The kill was entirely made with throwing sticks. Chief Sev watched the women and children welcome their returning men as always. With no wasted time, enough fresh meat was set aside for the evening fires. Other women took the rest to the smoking Ghers so it could be cured. It was as if this was the old way, even though none of this would have been possible just one winter ago.

The Chief thought pensively on these developments. He called a private meeting of the Elders and the Spearmaker. Once assembled in his Gher, he addressed them.

"Today I saw our hunters return with a huge elk in the dead of deep winter. I never thought this possible. We could never move this way in snow. Any meat we couldn't eat would spoil in a few days. Now the 'snow feet,' throwing sticks, and smoking meat allow us to hunt like wolves themselves. We can rain down darts from safer distance to kill. Now we store meat for entire moon cycles.

"There is a single reason for all this. The Eagle Feather's leadership saved the People. Bret also showed us the difference one man can make. This boy Emil, the way he thinks, is like none I've ever seen. He's also lucky. I want each of you to teach him your wisdom. Push him harder than any boy in the village. Make sure he develops the physical stamina required to lead. He's the Eagle Feather returned to the People.

"If he survives the warrior trials, Emil will be Chief following me. If I die before he comes of age, the Spearmaker will be Chief until his boy is ready. Do not tell Emil any of this. No one not here will know of this, until the time comes. I, Chief Sev of the Auroch People, have spoken."

Chapter Eighteen

Mammoth

"The lion may be king of the jungle but he knows, he shouldn't stand in the way of the elephant."
-Gujarati Proverb

THE HOWLING GRAY WOLVES woke the village. There was a brisk excitement in the shiny winter air. Emil had never seen a morning this busy. Mammoth. A single hunting team in "snow feet" was already speeding off in the direction of the howling.

Papa was cheerfully double-wrapping a heavy obsidian spearpoint. Cloud and Emil slowly staggered over. The boy was still brushing sleep from his eyes and squinting at the early sun's powerful glare off the snow. Papa's voice sang out.

"Mammoth, Babo! The wolves are calling us to the hunt! Have you ever heard them howl in daylight? They tell us mammoth are entering our valley from the Great Plains. The herds usually go through the granite cliffs of the Mountain Men, unless snow blocks the passes. They come in two to three days."

Emil announced, "Papa, I think the cave drawings show us a good way to hunt mammoth. There is another idea there, like they showed us the 'snow feet.'"

"Chief Sev knows mammoth best, let's go see him," Papa answered.

The Chief was seated on a hickory stump sharpening his spear. He puffed from his black pipe and greeted them warmly. "Good morning, young man, are you ready for mammoth?"

Emil had rarely spoken directly to the Chief before and was visibly nervous. Papa encouraged him. Emil took a deep breath. "My papa says mammoth are very dangerous. Chief, do the big bulls lead? What's the best way to kill one with a spear? I think the cave drawings also show us a safe way to hunt mammoth. Is there a huge tree somewhere on the path the mammoth take?"

The Chief's eyes sparkled with recollection.

"Yes, we call it the Old Man. It's the oldest tree in this valley and the biggest. Mammoth herds are led by an old female. The bulls bring up the rear when marching. They are very hard to kill with spears. A spot behind the ears or on top of the head and spine is best, but it's very hard to hit."

"Good," was the boy's laconic reply. Emil grabbed a branch and drew the entire cave drawing in the snow at the Chief's feet.

The two men looked at each other then back down at Emil. The boy's memory was incredible.

"Papa, it's good you noticed the cave drawings. The cave men drew a Falling Spear mammoth trap, not their spirits on the wall. This big old tree is right next to the mammoth path. There's a huge branch that goes high across the path. The cavemen hung a really big spear over this branch with a rope as a trap. This rope attaches back to the trunk of the big tree, then back across the path tied to another tree as high as a big bull mammoth's head. Anything smaller than a big mammoth passes safe under the rope. A bull mammoth has to push past the rope, which sets off the trap. The falling spear kills it."

The Chief motioned for them to sit down next to him. He took a knee and traced his finger back over the lines of the trap drawn in the snow. Smoke puffed slowly from his pipe as he closed his eyes in deep contemplation. Emil wasn't sure what to make of the look on the old warrior's face. Chief Sev grabbed his water pouch. "Impressive, most impressive. Let's go see the Old Man."

He led the four of them through a snow trail toward the Old Man. The pungent smell of smoke wafting from the Chief's pipe was strong and nutty in the crisp breeze.

"Do you smoke, Emil?" inquired the Chief with a raised eyebrow.

"No, my papa never has, Opa never did, and Papa says it's bad for breathing," was Emil's earnest reply. He didn't realize the Chief was joking.

The Chief chuckled, then wheezed back a dry smoker's cough. "Your papa's right, it's a filthy habit. Never smoke. Did you know your opa didn't think smoking was bad for breathing? Has your papa not told you the story of the Black Angel?"

Papa shook his head, and Emil was all ears. The Chief had the wistful faraway look in his eyes of a hunter who has seen too many harsh winters. He began.

"She was a pantheress, as black as the darkest night. We were at war with the Mountain Men and raiding their lands. This Black Angel wasn't a maneater, but a 'manhater.' She did this with increasing fury until the end. She did things normal panthers or even maneaters never do. She struck by both day and night. She never ate a bite of her victims and clawed up their bodies beyond recognition with rage.

"We later learned the reason for her fury. Two Mountain Men were out chopping wood and came across her cubs by her cave. They killed them. She saw this and avenged her babies by ambushing them. In the end the Black Angel wasn't evil, but a powerful, vengeful mother

"Your opa would lead four-man raiding teams into their lands. We'd swim the river during the full moon and hide in a cave on their side. Just before dawn we'd creep up and kill or snatch a guard and leave an eagle feather. We wore their footpads and instead of racing back across the river, we'd double back to this cave until the next night. They never figured this out. The Mountain Men thought they fought ghosts."

Emil stated, "You would leave an eagle feather to show them they weren't safe anywhere, even in their own village. We attacked their spirit."

Chief Sev nodded in agreement.

"Yes, wars only end when one side loses the will to fight. In war, attack your opponents' minds as well as their bodies. They wake up, one of their guards is lying dead with an eagle feather on his chest. The other is missing, never to be seen again, just as if he vanished into thin air. No one saw anything, no traces, and their warriors see no tracks back toward the river."

The Chief took another long drag from his pipe, while Emil pondered all of this, and continued.

"I was the youngest hunter on one such raid. We didn't know about the cub story until much later. We came across panther kills in the forest. It was just a maneater that was killing our enemy. We would find single Mountain Men torn to shreds on obscure trails.

"The Black Angel ambushed us from a tree shortly before dusk. I was the last in line and her target. Luck saved me! In her zeal to kill she missed seeing my spear hung over my shoulder and skewered herself in the side as she landed on me. With a bloody screeching roar, she instantly leapt back into a thorny hollow of trees. I was bruised but unhurt. We had to abort the raid and head back immediately. The whole forest had heard this ruckus.

"Your opa checked on me, then began following the blood trail into the brush to finish the panther. We protested. It was a war they started; let the panther kill more Mountain Men. The Eagle Feather knew this area was where their women and children pick fruit. He reminded us real men don't make war on women and children. They would be in danger from the wounded panther here tomorrow. We countered with him some of our women had been killed by Mountain Men. His rebuke of 'we are not those men' was no surprise. He could have ordered any of us after the panther but didn't. Respect is the currency of men, Emil. He treated us with respect."

Chief Sev looked so much younger recounting these events.

"The daylight was fading rapidly. My spear had started this mess. There was no way he was going in there after it without me. I suggested we wait a bit, maybe the cat would bleed out. I asked if there was time for a quick smoke before we went in. We never smoked on missions, it could get us killed. A whiff of smoke wouldn't matter now though, it was almost dark and we were leaving. He waited until I finished, then we followed the blood trail. There was dark blood everywhere. A child could have followed this trail. I led with him a step behind. We weren't that far in this wood when I felt a drop of something hot and wet on the back of my neck. We dove to the ground, looking up with our spears. The Black Angel was crouched to spring on us from a tree we'd just passed. She had bled out mere moments before we passed under her. Both of us had shaky hands as we looked into her lifeless eyes. We realized this panther had baited a trail with her own blood, then doubled back high in the trees to ambush us.

"This is when your opa asked, 'Who says smoking is bad for you?'" deadpanned the Chief.

Papa laughed hard. He'd clearly never heard this story from his father. They both thanked the old warrior.

The Chief's weathered face briefly lit up again with a youthful recollection. He looked Emil in the eye.

"We'd have followed your opa into Hell itself. He was truly a force of nature. I once saw him kill three huge Mountain Men so fast, all three were dead before the first hit the ground. Kishor was just...calm. This isn't why we loved him—he truly cared for us. Any danger, any risk he would take on himself first. Leadership is simple, Emil. First, know your stuff; second, be a man; third, take care of your men."

They were at the base of the Old Man by the hottest part of the day. The gnarled old colossus was the grandest thing Emil had ever seen. Papa and the Chief noted there were already notches in the timeless trunk of the ancient tree, at about the height of a bull mammoth's head.

Papa climbed the old tree and saw another notch in a smaller tree directly across the path. This was where the rope trigger was tied. *How many mammoths had this trap taken in days of old?*

Papa measured out loud, "The Falling Spear would have to be big, about the weight of two large men. If we double-wrapped some climbing ropes, they should hold it. We lace the rope in leaves and vines so it looks natural. How do we test this?"

Emil called out, "Papa, it works, otherwise the cavemen wouldn't have drawn it. The trap works."

The boy was right. It would take a full day to whittle a tree trunk down into the Falling Spear. At least four men were needed to climb the tree and set the trap.

Papa assessed, "We can be back at dawn with ropes and axes and have the trap set by dusk. I'll mark a good tree for the falling spear close by, before we leave. We might miss this herd though."

Chief Sev shrugged. "There will be herds passing for at least a full moon cycle. If this trap works, we can take a bull from every passing mammoth herd without losing a single hunter. That would leave us with enough smoked meat to last through spring. This is incredible."

The old warrior took another puff of his pipe. Emil saw him face the sun and hold his arm out. His hand was thumb up, fingers touching, with his palm facing his eyes. Chief Sev had placed his hand so the sun sat on his first finger. Emil looked at Papa in confusion. The Chief and Papa grinned. It was easy to forget how young the boy was.

"Emil, pay attention," Papa instructed. "This could save you someday.'

The gap between the sun and the ground was exactly the height of Chief Sev's four fingers.

"Emil, this is how we measure remaining daylight. We all know how long it takes a man to run from the Mountain River to the village. That distance is roughly four fingers running, or eight fingers walking. The animals rule the night. You must always know when the sun sets. Do you follow?"

Emil pondered this, then smiled. "I think what you are saying is this. This Old Man tree is about halfway between the village and the Mountain River. I think it would take two fingers running to get home before sunset, or four fingers walking. The space is four fingers now, so if we want to walk home before sunset, we'd better leave now?"

The men's smiles told him he was right. Emil remembered to thank Chief Sev for this lesson.

At the evening meal, the scouts reported the mammoths would take two days to get to the area of the trap. Early the next morning Aash and two hunting teams headed for the Old Man. They found the spear tree Aash had marked and chopped it down. By midday the log was whittled down into the heavy Falling Spear. The team sharpened the point and tempered it with fire. The sun was high when strong lengths of sinewy rope had finally hoisted everything into place.

The final step was disguising the rope with vines and branches. The Falling Spear mammoth trap was set. Now there was nothing to do but wait. Aash and the hunting teams were back well before sunset.

There was just something grand about the giant pachyderms. The People were eager to see if the new trap would work. All the little boys wanted to go see the mammoth hunt, yet none were allowed. If things went bad, mammoth were still the largest, most dangerous game in the woods. It was no place for children.

The plan was simple. At dawn two hunting teams and a group of village women would take position on a series of small hills a short distance from the Old Man. If the trap was sprung, there would be a great deal of meat to skin and pack back to the village on travois. Chief Sev still marveled at the notion of taking a mammoth with a trap. It couldn't be this easy.

There were no wolf tracks or sign anywhere near the trail to the ancient redwood, but Papa knew the wolves were watching closely. Everything was in place by mid-morning. *If you have a good plan, the hardest part is usually just sitting and waiting.*

As always, Cloud was the first to know. The white wolf's keen nose picked up the mammoth scent well before the hunters saw the herd approaching the Old Man. It was a small herd led by a dark gray spotted female. The forest sounds of the winter birds were replaced by a cacophony of snorting cows, crying calves, and the lazy grunts of the bull mammoths.

Aash watched the herd from a small tree on an adjacent hill. He checked the wind to make sure the herd's keen noses wouldn't suspect anything. Watching the herd brought a tinge of sadness. *I understand now why you didn't hunt mammoth, Father. It's the sounds they make back and forth, and the way they scold and tease the playful calves. All of it just seems so...human.*

His thoughts were interrupted by an abrupt snapping sound followed immediately by a thundery clap. Flocks of small birds fled the trees around the Old Man. There was an earsplitting bellow from the mammoth that triggered the trap. Aash could see an old bull down on his knees with his ears flopped forward and his trunk folded. It was a clean kill to the spine. The force of the blow had actually forced an ivory tusk clean out of its socket. The herd was angry. Several bulls surrounded the fallen mammoth. The herd was stomping angrily in a killing rage. They trumpeted harsh-voiced grunts over their companion's fate. They weren't leaving the old bull.

The hunters waited while not sure what to do. It was the wolves that solved this stalemate. The large gray pack strutted into view, stiff-legged and snarling at the herd. Ever so slowly with great reservation, the spotted old cow slowly turned and resumed down the trail. Chief Sev and Aash couldn't believe their eyes, as many of the herd touched heads with the fallen bull before they left. There weren't many dry eyes among the People now.

Aash led them to the trail quickly. Few things are as pitiful looking as a dead mammoth.

The Chief spoke sagely. "This kill is good for the People. We need all this meat and fat to survive the winter. The tusks make us so may tools, splints, needles, knives. We honor this old bull, and will use every part of him. Let's get to work. We have so much to do to be home by nightfall."

The People loaded eight full travois that day. A heaping treasure of meat, fat, and gleaming ivory tusks. As the weary caravan made its way home, they could hear the cracking of bones and marrow on the trail behind them. The wise wolves were finally claiming their grisly spoils.

Chapter Nineteen
Edelweiss

"The child of lion is a lion."
-Swahili Proverb

BLUE SMOKE ROSE LAZILY from the village Ghers at the cherry red dawn. Spring was reborn in all her majestic, verdant grandeur. She decreed new life must burst forth from the death and cold of frost and snow. It had been the best winter the People could remember. The smoked mammoth meat kept them well fed. Chief Sev and the Elders couldn't remember such a winter. None had died from hunger or the frosty elements.

Mama and Holly were walking the children through the morning dew droplets. They listened to the melodious chirps of freshly hatched birds. Holly pointed out the geese honking high overhead on their return north. Holly was the midwife for the People and Mama's dearest friend. She'd helped deliver Emil into the world with the ancient scarf method. Emil knew his papa only referred to her as "that Angel Holly" in honor of this service.

The People taught their young ones to swim. A boisterous little band was headed for a lily filled little pond. Cloud was up front chasing yellow butterflies as the smell of lilac filled the breeze.

Mama was telling them all a story about Lake Nakuru in the jungles of the south lands beyond the great sand seas. The legend was, there are so many flamingos there, the lake looks pink from a distance. The children marveled at the idea of a pink lake.

Despite this pleasant setting, Mama had a strange feeling of trepidation. Experience had shown her the value of this sixth sense, but she couldn't quite put a finger on it. A child wanted to know if they could swim with flamingos, or if there were crocodiles?

Mama laughed. "I think so. I've never been there but its's supposed to be salty water. The crocodiles there like fresh water."

"There aren't any crocs in our little swimming pond, right?" asked Shala.

The two women reassured their charges there weren't. The pond was still very chilly and Cloud splashed them all jumping in after the two women. The little ones now wanted no part of the cold water.

Mama pointed out how Cloud swam paddling with his paws and told the children to do the same. There were still no takers.

Finally, Mama offered to tell a favorite story about a river turtle and a Skorpon if they all tried swimming. The children loved her stories and took this deal. The woman took two in at a time until every child had a turn. Some were naturally better than others. Emil was in the latter camp. He hated getting his hair wet and was scared of having his head underwater.

The older boys began teasing him. Jak went a bit too far. "How are you going to be a hunter, Emil, if you're so scared of just water?" taunted the older boy.

Emil ignored him as the ribbing got worse, then Emil lost his temper. "I will learn to swim, Jak. You can never grow more brains, Jak. You will always be an idiot!" Emil fired back.

The bigger boy pushed him. Emil punched him in the face and the boys wrestled until Jak had pinned Emil into submission. Jak won but never picked on Emil again. The People let their children settle such differences. How would a child who couldn't handle a bully grow into a hunter that faced down a charging Grizzly?

"If you two baboons are finished, it's time for the story," declared Mama. Then she started.

"A long time ago there was a wise old turtle who lived next to a great river. He was kind and often advised the forest creatures. The Skorpon came to the riverbank asking for a ride to the other side.

"Midway across the river, the compassionate turtle survives the Skorpon's sting due to his protective shell. The turtle is baffled by the Skorpon's behavior. They are old friends. Both also know the Skorpon can't swim, and a stinger can't penetrate a turtle shell. The Skorpon responds that it acted not out of malice but an irresistible urge to sting, even if it drowns. The wise old turtle is angry, but ultimately decides against drowning the Skorpon. However, the old turtle never helps him again. The turtle then thanks the Sky Spirits for this valuable lesson."

The children all hooted at this. "That Skorpon was so dumb!" laughed Mats.

"Despite his wisdom, so was the turtle," Mama replied to a chorus of confused faces. "He got very lucky. He should've known a Skorpon is a Skorpon. It will always live up to its nature."

The weather warmed as spring gave way to summer. In time, the daily treks to the chilly little lily pond resulted in every child of the People showing basic swimming ability. Each could at least paddle like a wolf through the water.

A moon cycle later, the swimming group was walking back from the pond at midday. The little boys were arguing which was more dangerous, lions or tigers. The little girls just rolled their eyes at this. They all asked Mama to judge. Lulu was pondering a good answer, when she made the deadly mistake of stepping over instead of onto a small log in their path.

Mama's painful gasp snapped Emil and Cloud to attention. Holly caught Mama as she wobbled, reaching for her foot. Emil was horrified, thinking, *No, no, not another snake, no please!*

Holly brushed a squashed red Skorpon from under Mama's foot. Lulu was quivering as the pain and poison hit in waves, convulsing her body. Holly and the boys gently laid her down in the shade for comfort. Her skin was pale and her breathing was becoming labored.

Mama took Emil's hand in hers, smiling for him, despite the tears from the pain.

"It's all right, Babo, it's my time. I love you, watch over Papa." Then her breathing slowed, and she gently closed her eyes.

Emil's mind was racing at full speed. Mama was unconscious but still breathing. Edelweiss! *There's still a bit of time.*

Emil told Holly, "Keep her alive, get Papa and the healers. We need edelweiss!"

Before Holly could answer, Emil and his white wolf were crashing through the forest back toward the Mountain River.

They reached the sandy banks of the Mountain River as fast as the boy could move. Emil panted, catching his breath as he studied the current. *I'm not a good swimmer. The current seemed calm today, but it's stronger than it looks. There is no time. I need a small log or something, anything to help float across.*

Cloud saw Emil staring across the river and barked at him. Then the white wolf also glanced across the river and barked twice. Emil understood. He placed his arm over the wolf's neck and pointed at the opposite bank. He led the wolf into the shallows, wrapping his arms tightly around Cloud's neck. The pair were swept downriver by the current. Both paddled furiously across the river, as the white wolf kept the determined young boy afloat.

The intrepid duo was exhausted as they crawled ashore the sand of the opposite bank. Emil had swallowed a lot of water, which he violently threw up, but they made it.

Emil needed Inga. *I don't know where the Mountain Man village is. It's strange thick forest ahead of us. Papa said we watch each other for war. I'll bring them here to me!*

Soon, the unmistakable smoke from a large raging signal fire was rising into the clear blue sky for all to see. The still dripping boy had made several trips into nearby brush for kindling. Emil built the blaze in the sand. Then he forced himself to do the breathing exercise while he waited.

It wasn't long before Cloud sniffed the air and barked at something approaching rapidly out of the woods. Four large, shaggy Mountain Men were watching them through the trees. The men had incredulous looks on their faces.

Emil began frantically jumping up and down screaming. "Inga, Inga, Inga, Mama, Skorpon, edelweiss! Skorpon, edelweiss!"

The hunting team approached him cautiously, wary of a trap. They saw the boy was alone save for the white wolf. One of the Mountain Men was the biggest man Emil had ever seen, a mountain in a red beard. The boy kept pleading.

The big man squinted his eyes in disbelief, asking, "Inga?" Clearly all four men had seen Cloud before.

Emil pointed back over their heads toward their village, "Inga, Inga," he pleaded. The boy clawed at his foot, mimicking a clawing bite. "Skorpon, Skorpon, Mama." Emil pointed at their leather pouches. "Edelweiss! Edelweiss!' The boy made the taking motion with his palm.

The message was clear. Aki turned to the other hunters, while saying in their language, "This must be Aash's boy. Why else would the great wolf follow him? They need edelweiss. A Skorpon has bit one of them."

The huge hunter knelt slowly in front of Emil, smiling and flashing the peace sign. "Edelweiss?" he asked. "Edelweiss?"

Emil was frantically jumping up and down, motioning *yes, give it to me*.

The big man placed his mighty ivory axe on the ground. He was looking for a small leather wrapping in his deerskin pouch.

Sharp words ringing from the smallest man of the team interrupted him. The big man turned horrified at what he was hearing. He shook his head violently at the smaller man. Emil had no idea what they were saying, but the tone was menacing and the argument fierce.

Emil couldn't understand their words. Vili was telling the others this was a clear breach of the peace treaty. The boy was a spy sent by the People. His story didn't matter. They had the right to kill him and the wolf.

Cloud sensed this, and the rumblings of a low growl started in his throat. The ferocious white wolf stepped in front of Emil. Fenrir in full effect. It was once again clear to all present the wolf's focus had unfinished business with Vili's throat. The little boy slowly drew his obsidian knife. Emil tried to look fierce, or as fierce as an innocent child can look when trying to appear intimidating.

Aki thundered at Vili, "How black is your soul, man? This is just a boy! One who swam the river alone, by the way. He's trying to get edelweiss to save someone. His father saved my Inga! Let's give it to him as long as he leaves now!" *I should just let the wolf have him*, thought Aki.

Vili just raised his lethal ivory war axe in response. Aki turned and intensely asked Emil something. It was as if he was desperately offering something to Emil while nodding yes. Emil thought he was offering the edelweiss for payment. The crying boy offered up his obsidian knife, holding it up as if in trade. Emil nodded yes to Aki.

Then three things happened at once. First, Cloud's snarls focused on Vili. Second, the cruel hunter raised his mighty ivory war axe to kill the wolf. Third, neither of the first two things mattered much. In a flash, Aki had slammed his forearm down thunderously on Vili, completely shattering the smaller man's arm. He picked Vili up over his head, as if he were but a small child, and unceremoniously hurled him back in a heap toward the woods.

The red-bearded giant raised his mighty war axe. He bellowed fiercely at the remaining two Mountain Men in their tongue. "You both witnessed the boy accept my guest invitation, yes? By sacred law, he is now under Aki's protection. Is this a problem?"

The pair of Mountain Men looked at each other, then at the senseless Vili lying in a tangle like a drowned rat, not two paces away from them. Neither could well disguise the disdain they had for the fallen hunter. Truth be told, they were both fathers and decent fellows. Even if they weren't, both were keenly aware of what a truly dangerous man Aki was. A Grizzly itself couldn't have been as intimidating as the angry fire now radiating from the giant's sharp green eyes. Emil shuddered involuntarily.

One hunter just shrugged, saying, "The guest law is sacred. Get the boy out of here with the edelweiss."

The other Mountain Man nodded, saying something along the lines of, "Use the boat to help him back."

Cloud intuitively sensed all of this and stopped growling. Aki took a knee and his rage was replaced by a kind father's smile. He pointed to himself, "Aki, Aki, Aki," then he held up the leather wrap. "Edelweiss!" he exclaimed. Aki motioned for the boy to follow him up the shore. Cloud was still growling a bit, as the two other men saw to the unconscious one, but Emil stopped this. They quickly followed the giant.

Aki led them to a large hollowed-out log hidden behind the tree line. The big man carried this log overhead to the edge of the river and lightly jumped in. He motioned for Emil and Cloud to hop in, which they did. Aki paddled them back across to their side in no time. He handed Emil the edelweiss wrapping and pointed toward the People's village. "Go," he smiled. The giant watched the little boy and his wolf racing through the sand into their forest, before the log even came to a full stop on the shore.

Shortly before dusk, a panting, exhausted Emil burst into the healers' Gher yelling. "Edelweiss! Mama! Edelweiss!"

Mama was lying asleep on a sleeping fur while Papa held her hand. The healers changed the wet poultice on her forehead. Papa's exhausted eyes were red and bloodshot. He stared at a mud-splattered Emil as if in a dream. His son was dirty and completely scratched up from thorns. Papa thought, *The hunting teams we sent to find him must have brought him back.*

"Papa, it's really me,' declared Emil as he turned to the healers. "The Mountain Men gave me edelweiss. First, we grind it up and spread it on the bite. Then we put some in water for Mama to drink. Hurry!"

The healers looked warily at the dried white flower in suspicion. *The Mountain Men could not be trusted.* Lulu's breathing was growing fainter. This was just too much for Papa. He snatched it from them and ground up four flowers on the grinding stone. Papa took Mama's foot and doused the cut with the powder. Papa and Emil woke Mama up and made her drink deeply from the water laced with the edelweiss. Then came the hard part. Papa and Emil waited all night next to Mama, trying to keep her comfortable.

Emil fell asleep in Papa's arms and woke up to his father's hoarse jubilant yells. Mama's fever had broken. There was no more pain; she was very sore but conscious. Mama sat up from the sleeping furs asking, "How did I get here, boys?" They both smothered her with kisses.

The healers stampeded back into the Gher to fuss over her and told Papa he must sleep now.

Papa carried an exhausted Emil to their Gher while the boy told his tale of the river crossing, Aki, and the hollowed log. It was an incredible story, and Papa would think on it later. Once back in the privacy of their Gher, he held Babo fiercely to his chest and sobbed deep tears of relief.

Mama was on her feet again by midday. She was well enough to nibble at the evening meal. As the story spread, the entire village of the People was in awe of Emil and his white wolf. Chief Sev just blissfully rolled his eyes up toward the Sky Spirits and shook his head in utter amazement.

Chapter Twenty
Star Talk

"Death was afraid of him because he had the heart of a lion."
-Gurkha Proverb

THE LARGE GHER FILLED to capacity as the glowing summer sun baked the entire valley. Chief Sev fiddled with his pipe, and decided to put it away. Three Elders set out fresh sliced fruit and water. The Gher flaps were left open for light and fresh air.

Papa brought Emil in, and he looked up at his father a bit confused. The Elders greeted them warmly and offered them some fruit. Emil settled in Papa's lap, eyed a peach, and began noisily munching away.

Chief Sev stated, "How is your mama, Emil? Peaches are my favorite too. Young man, we have some questions for you."

"Good," replied the boy. "Mama is watching the girls sort berries."

Chief Sev cleared his throat and reminded himself to speak in a gentle tone.

"Emil, yesterday was an incredible day. The edelweiss saved your mama. No one has ever survived a Skorpon bite before. The People are proud of you. Some of yesterday still mystifies us. Where did you get the white flower? Is it possible the Mountain Woman forgot or left us that leather wrapping here in the village?"

"No, Chief," stated Emil, "a Mountain Man named Aki gave it to me yesterday."

"What did this Mountain Man look like?" softly questioned the Chief.

"He was a giant! The biggest man I've ever seen. Aki had red hair and carried a big axe with sharp white bones. He's the scariest man in the world, but he was very nice. He stopped the smaller hunter from hurting me." revealed Emil.

The Chief was listening intently. He looked over the boy's shoulder at Papa, whose emphatic nod fully confirmed this description of Aki. Chief Sev went on.

"I see, and this Aki, this is very important, Emil. When Aki gave you this edelweiss, were the Mountain Men on our side of the river? We must know this?"

"No," Emil declared. He paused for a second. "Mama explained territory to me once. They were not here. I got the white flowers on their side of the river?"

The Elders had a quizzical look. The chief turned his head, took a deep breath and smiled wryly. "Emil, can you please tell me exactly how you got over to their lands again, and young man, be careful. Because after yesterday, if you tell us you can actually fly, I might believe you."

Papa remarked, "Emil, please just tell them the whole story again from the start."

The boy took a big gulp of water, then repeated the entire tale again. Afterwards, the boy looked back at Papa, then Chief Sev. "May I have that big plum too?" Emil asked.

Four sets of hands fumbled over the same plum as they gave it to the boy. Papa's eyes were moist and red again as he hugged Emil tight. Chief Sev smiled in thoughtful silence. *Emil's story matched known facts and was consistent in retellings.*

"An old graybeard like me has seen some amazing things, good and bad. This might be the best," stated Chief Sev. "You mentioned a snakelike man. Snakes are evil."

"Were they bad to you too?" asked Emil in a small, inquisitive voice.

"The striped boas," shuddered the Chief, "it still gives me nightmares, so I don't talk of it."

"Emil," reminded Papa sternly, "We don't ask another man his business unless he cares to reveal it. Remember?"

"Yes," apologized Emil, "I'm sorry, Chief."

Chief Sev's eyes were far away. He shuddered again then sighed while taking a deep breath.

"No, Spearmaker. Emil asks a fair question. We've been questioning the lad all morning, and he can handle it. Back during war, I was sent to set traps for the Mountain Men on their trails. I'd been watching them all day and knew I'd spend the night on their side of the river. I found a heavily wooded hill with a cozy-looking cave. It was a bright night, though rain seemed possible. There was nothing but a bunch of sleeping bats in the cave. Something just felt wrong. I decided to pass the moonlight night up in a tree instead.

"At the false dawn, I saw something I'll never forget. A pack of large striped boas had sealed off the cave entrance. They were feasting on the trapped, screaming bats. The huge snakes were hunting as a pack! They coordinated their movements so there was no place for a single bat to escape. Snakes aren't pack hunters! I could have been lying sleeping in that cave! It still gives me nightmares."

Everyone else in the Gher reacted to this serpentine tale in mute white-knuckled horror.

"You were so brave, Chief Sev. You went in alone just like Bret," Emil observed. The Chief just waved this notion away.

Later that day, Emil and Papa were sitting under an old cherry tree on the edge of the village. The sun was as high as it would get that day and scalding the ground below. Emil was cuddled in Papa's lap. They were sipping water in the shade. This was a "Man Talk," where Emil and his papa talked man to man. The serious look in Emil's eyes at this tender age always made Papa chuckle inwardly. However, what his boy had just pulled off was nothing to scoff at.

Emil was chattering away about cherry trees. "I think it's the best tree, Papa. The fruit is so good, and nothing is prettier than all those blossoms in the spring."

Papa pondered this. "You're right, Babo. I never thought of it like that. The ancients honor this tree and its beautiful blossoms. They considered a short beautiful life, such as that of a cherry blossom, to be ideal."

Papa explained.

"The People are tough and resilient; life requires this. We only honor courage in death. The sole honor for a man is death in service. He died in battle. For a woman, we only honor death in childbirth. It's just the old way. I don't agree with this. There is more to life than a good death.

"Your actions at the river saved Mama. Do you know how you really did it?"

Emil was wondering if Papa had gotten a bit too much sun. Papa laughed at the puzzled look in his son's eyes.

"Oh, I know you took bold actions. The process you used was developing the situation. It's good to plan ahead, but life rarely goes to plan. Any experienced hunter would have rightly disagreed with the risk of your plan. The river is rough. The Mountain Men are dangerously unpredictable, and setting a fire in their land could start a war. The elders would have talked you out of it. For the most part, who could blame them? But Mama would have died."

Emil tilted his head. "I know, I didn't know how to do it, I was scared, but I had to save her."

Papa continued.

"On the other hand, expertise comes from experience. This is a nice way of saying someone has already made the mistakes you are about to make. The pattern is always a bit different, but they've seen something close before. Bret was our best fisherman. If we needed to rely on fishing for food, it would be foolish and potentially costly to ignore his local expertise and advice.

"There is a delicate balance here, Babo. Developing the situation is when you listen to the experts but not too much. It's when you have a strategy, but adapt it to the inevitable uncertainty of local circumstances. When you went for the edelweiss, Emil, you instinctively developed the situation. Remember this.

"Mama is alive today, because of your memory, courage, mindset, and a bit of luck. We can only control three of these things, Emil. You took great risk, but only because the reward was greater. This is a good mindset."

As they walked back to their Gher, Papa asked a bit too casually, "Babo, this smaller Mountain Man who was going to hurt you, did he have gray eyes like a snake?"

"Yes, Papa, have you met him too?" asked Emil.

Papa's face hardened into a Stygian mask. "He'd best pray I never do again," swore Papa in a hard, chilling voice Emil had never heard before.

Papa noticed Emil had jumped a step back. He smiled warmly and took a deep breath. "I'm sorry if I scared you, son. Men shouldn't hurt little boys," added Papa, his voice back to normal.

"I'm not so little, Papa," smiled Emil. "Mama was telling me about animals up in the stars at night; can we see them?'

"That's a great idea, Babo, we'll go tonight. Let's get our daily tasks done and take a nap."

"I know we usually talk man to man up in the trees at night. Can we bring Mama too tonight?" Emil asked.

Papa chuckled. "It's not a Man Talk, Babo. Of course, we'll bring Mama too, it'll be a Star Talk!"

The little family was oohing and aahing as the shimmering silver star shot across the vast immenseness of black sky above. They were sitting on the wooden platform Papa had fixed high up their favorite "night tree." The dark night forest extended downhill in every direction and toward the river.

Mama was pointing at a particularly bright glowing star.

"Babo, that is the north star. When you see this star it's always north. Then you know the other directions."

"Where are the star animals?" asked Emil.

Papa relaxed against the trunk with his hands clasped behind his head. Mama began tracing the sky with Emil's finger in her hand.

"There is Ursa, a little bear. See, starting from the North Star. Over there is Leo the sky lion. See its head and body? Here is Orion the hunter of the sky, a man, see him? OK, and finally over there is a great bull Taurus. See the long horns?"

Emil imagined all of these majestic creatures glowing far away in the heavens above. *Are they truly the Sky Spirits of our ancestors? Do they really watch us in eternal silence from so high above?* This is a nice thought.

"This is so nice! I wish Cloud could see them too! Is there a sky wolf too, Mama?" Emil asked.

Mama turned him around and pointed out Lupus the Wolf to the south.

Cloud had howled and whined in protest at being left behind in the village.

"Let's hope Cloud doesn't leave us a 'special present' back in the Gher in protest. That wolf really wanted to come along," chuckled Papa.

Mama replied rosily, "Cloud has saved all of us so many times. I'm still amazed how you two crossed the river. If he poohs in the Gher so be it, we can clean it. But he won't."

She wrapped her arms around them both." Thank you for saving me, Babo. It was incredibly brave!"

"I didn't have time to be scared, Mama; well, not until it was over," admitted Emil.

Papa reflected on this.

It's true. Life is hard for the People. The hunters honor courage and ridicule cowardice. Both are actually a function of the circumstances and luck. A man could fight for his survival or his loved ones if attacked. He'd be brave if his spear strikes true, and possibly if there was no time to run or think. Clearly the outcome mattered. Papa decided the bravery was in the sacrifice, not the outcome. This realization was enough to keep anyone humble.

However, what Emil had done was truly brave. Anyone who knowingly puts themselves in harm's way to save another soul, with utter disregard for their own fate, this is the epitome of courage.

Aash watched Lulu and Emil peacefully cuddled together under the stars next to him. He looked up at the night sky, thinking of something his own father had told him long ago.

"Do good with no expectations."

Papa now truly understood the power of this belief. The Eagle Feather had been a great man.

I understood you better, Father, now that I have a son myself. Greatness is defined by the impact of a person's actions, for the better of the People. Greatness isn't perfection; all of us are flawed in our own ways. Yet this potential for something greater perpetually lies within, if we have courage.

The next day started out in normal fashion. The skies were clear and the sun made his usual appearance, as the People went about their daily tasks. The women fixed the Ghers and gathered berries and nuts. The children, escorted by Cloud and Mama, found time to joke, tease, and run. The boys hunted eggs and gathered kindling. Papa worked on crafting and reshaping damaged spearpoints. The hunting teams had success in making meat.

It was the best part of the day again. The People rested, joked, and sang, while the savory meat roasted over the fires. There was just the start of a bit of dancing when Chief Sev and the Elders approached Emil's family in unison. The Chief held his hands up for silence and the drumming stopped. He motioned for Emil to step forward. The boy did so cautiously, wondering if he was in trouble again.

Chief Sev addressed the People.

"The Eagle Feather meant a great deal to the People. All of you, young and old, have heard the tales. All of us graybeards witnessed them firsthand. Emil, what you did the other day was an act unlike anything we've seen since your opa. He served as an inspiration for the People. You took reckless risks, young man. Learn and think carefully on this going forward. Yet life is but one reckless risk. You give the People hope."

Chief Sev produced an intricately weaved buckskin headband holding a single magnificent eagle father and placed it on Emil's forehead. The band had Bret's jumping fish pattern and the feather was a beautiful snow white.

"The Eagle Feather has returned to the People!" he proclaimed in a joyful voice. The People cheered.

Emil wore the Eagle Feather from that day forward.

Chapter Twenty-One
The Purple Fruit

ONE LAZY, HAZY SUMMER morning Emil and the village boys were out hunting bird eggs in the warm reddish-orange sunlight. They were all pointing out Emil's near empty basket. While he stared at the red sky, they good-naturedly teased about how horribly bad Emil was at finding eggs.

Truth be told, the boys had a point. Emil would've been the first to admit he was bored silly by bird egg hunting. However, this was a daily task for the boys. Emil could just hear Papa's voice reminding him, *We do our duty.*

There were, in fact, two solid reasons that any bird eggs in the valley were usually safe if Emil was hunting them. The first, which he'd readily admit, was after Dori he was constantly watching over his friends in rocky, low bushy terrain. The boy accepted his parents' explanation that snakes were just like any other creature trying to survive.

Emil knew this was true; despite this, the fact was he still hated snakes and always would. Papa had drilled into his head that killing is only for food or defense. Emil didn't kill anything unnecessarily, but he was always alert for snakes.

I think of you often, Bret. I'm grateful for all your lessons, especially on snakes. I remember you told me snakes kill more People, even great hunters, than any other forest creature. This is so true. Tigers or panthers mainly avoid us. Bears also usually steer clear of the village. It's easy to avoid berry bushes in Grizzly country. Snakes, though, are everywhere around us. They are a threat day or night, hard to see, and lethal. Since Dori's passing, snake bite has taken four more of the People.

So, while the other boys were focused on eggs, Emil and Cloud kept silent watch over his friends. Emil had trained his white wolf to point out snakes as well. The boy had become skilled at subtly influencing or actually directing his boys away from risky snake areas without a direct word. There was an unspoken truth, which the boys now all subconsciously acknowledged. They followed Emil. He was their leader now, even the older boys.

The second reason, which was also unspoken common knowledge among the People, was that Emil's mind was special. Chief Sev had presented him with a rare Grizzly bear claw necklace after he'd discovered the Falling Spear mammoth trap. The Falling Spear had taken eight mammoths for the People at the sole cost of four broken ropes and one deep cut to a hand from meat skinning.

The Chief and Elders taught Emil all sorts of things and pushed him hard. He still performed the required daily tasks. Papa and Mama made sure none of this went to Emil's head. They didn't actually need to. Like his opa before him, Emil was fiercely devoted to the People. Whenever he was asked to do more than the others, Emil simply replied, "Good."

He was asked to always run one more lap than the other boys. Good. He had to learn all of the People's knowledge, skills, traditions and history. Good. Good. Good.

Most importantly, the Chief and Elders had all asked him where and how he came up with all these creative ideas. "My papa told me imagination is the most important skill for a hunter," Emil replied.

Emil described how sometimes he'd just sit quietly between chores and imagine adventures and think about things. He'd remember something and try to imagine a solution. Mostly though, as he went about his days and nights, it was just always there in the back of his mind. Emil was always imagining and asking, *Why or why not?*

Chief Sev had emphatically told Emil, in front of Papa, to do as much imagining as possible and to always share any ideas or questions he came up with.

Emil was actually doing both these things just now. As he scanned for snakes, for some reason he was thinking of the bending throwing sticks on the cave wall drawings.

I remember that really windy winter day just before the great winter hailstorm. That Gher binding snapped and sent a rock flying clear out of the village into the forest. Could the bent throwing sticks in the drawing actually be some sort of rock throwing pouch? I should talk to Papa about this.

Chuckles around him snapped him back to the present. Emil smiled and looked down at the single egg in his pouch and laughed. "Good, more baby birds will survive to be born!" He realized he was daydreaming and tried to focus on finding at least a few more eggs.

The boys were under strict orders not to veer too far away on their own. They'd inadvertently strayed away anyway, nearly reaching the river as they jostled and kidded around.

Cloud had wandered off, chasing birds by the river. The white wolf came back with a new purple fruit and dropped it at Emil's feet. None of the boys had seen this fruit before. Emil picked it up and sniffed it. "Let's see if it's good," said Mats.

Emil drew his obsidian knife, pausing for a second thinking of Bret, then deftly sliced the purple fruit in half. It smelled wonderful. The fragrant juices dripped down the black blade onto his little fingers.

He was just about to take a bite when he remembered Mama's story about the deadly yew berry seeds. "No!" insisted Emil. "We have to take it back to the village first to see if someone knows if it's safe to eat."

"C'mon, Emil, the village is a full walk away. It smells so good! Look, the birds seem to be eating them too," argued Mats. The other boys chimed hungrily in as well in support.

"Mats," explained Emil gently, "this is a second mistake. Our first one was not staying next to the village like we're supposed to. What if it's just like the mistake we made with the bears at the river? It could be poisonous like the pretty yew berry seeds. Let's just run home and eat it after asking."

Mats went pale at this memory and nodded quietly. "Yeah, let's not make a second mistake." Then the speedy boy promptly tore into a sprint. "Last one home's a rotten egg!"

The race home was on with glee.

At the village, Emil showed this purple fruit to Mama. "This is a prugna," explained Mama. "They are very rare and yummy. It's Papa's favorite." Mama cut the fruit into small pieces, so each of the children got a taste.

"There is none left for Papa now, can we go back and look for more?" asked Emil.

Mama nodded. "Prugna grow on a tree, we will go find it after noon chores."

Lulu, Emil, and Cloud went to find the prugna tree. "We will surprise Papa. He will love this!" revealed Mama.

Emil giggled. "Papa always says love is in the little things Mama. Does he mean love comes from prugna?"

"No," smirked Mama with a twinkle in her eye. "He means love is the little kind things we do for one another." As they followed Cloud into the forest, Mama marveled at the conversations a child of so few winters was capable of.

They finally found the massive prugna tree in a clearing close to the river. Cloud was chasing a flock of birds he had flushed. Emil cheerfully plucked the ripe fruit while chatting away. "Mama, did you know Papa was scared of you?"

"What?" asked Mama. For some reason, Lulu had that same bad feeling from the pond again. Mama smiled and cut two pieces of smoked venison from her leather pouch. She offered one to her son, taking the other for herself.

"Papa taught me special breathing to do when something is scary, like hunting a bear. He did it before your first dance," Emil explained.

Cloud all of a sudden yipped and flushed two white rabbits and bounded after them toward the river. They watched the rabbits dodge sideways at just the right instant as Cloud went flying by. The wolf was a bit confused deciding which rabbit to chase. The larger rabbit disappeared into bushes by the river, with Cloud in hot pursuit. They laughed at the puzzled look on Cloud's face.

They were thirsty from the long walk and salty smoked meat. Emil began filling his water pouch in the river. He heard a sudden rapid flutter of wings behind him. A flock of startled birds scattered south from the dark tree line by the river. The wind shifted again.

Emil sniffed the wind, stepping protectively in front of Mama, drawing his black knife at once.

Mama sprang alert, instantly leveling her obsidian-tipped light spear. "Get behind me!" she ordered. Lulu saw tawny, menacing death slithering low into the clearing. *The Sabretooth*.

The one-eyed cat is smiling wickedly at us, thought Lulu. The big cat had them now, and could take his own sweet time. *The prugna tree is closest. We can't reach it in time. I'll buy Emil the time.*

Mama looked straight and hard into the visceral malevolence of those immense yellow eyes. Lulu's voice was loud and clear.

"Babo, when I say run, you will climb the prugna tree as fast as you can. You will stay there no matter what happens until Papa comes, DO YOU UNDERSTAND?"

Emil knew this tone in her voice. Mama's gentle eyes had a fierce icy blue glow he'd never seen before. "Yes, Mama," he responded. The big cat came for them with a blood-curdling roar.

As Emil had just now discovered, Lulu of the cheerful blue eyes, who'd endured the pain of childbirth with joyful indifference. She who loved to dance to the People's drums and chant stories with the best of the Elders. She who everyone agreed knew more songs than existed, and caroled countless lovely lullabies to her baby. She, the one who rosily sang through life with carefree joy, comforting all the People's children with tender empathy.

For all of that, Lulu, like most truly gentle souls, was also a woman of savage temperament when provoked. She saw the sinister slits of the Sabretooth's eyes and the unholy wickedness radiating within. As deadly a killer as there was in the world, was coming for her baby. This brought the savage deep within her boiling to the surface. Lulu commanded, "Run, Emil!"

Mama took a step, leveling her spear, then flew forward like the blue-eyed angel of death herself, meeting the Sabretooth's charge with her own. Lulu sang out the ancient battle cry of the People with an unbridled fury, known only to the female of the order, and the deadly determination seen only in mothers of any species defending their cub.

"HAR HAR MAHADEV!"

Chapter Twenty-Two
The Gift

"Do not try to fight a lion if you are not one yourself."
-Byzantine Proverb

Aash was tempering a stubborn spear point near dusk at the first thunderclap. He recalled the tormentous scarlet tint to the sky that morning. His belly grumbled. *Fresh meat tonight for a change would be good.* The hunters returned early with great trepidation and no meat. Chief Sev called a quick council of the People. His voice was deep with emotion.

"The Sabretooth has returned. The hunters report fresh tracks by the river, it has definitely killed. It storms tonight with the new moon. We'll post night guards. No one leaves the village alone. Make sure there are two hunters with the women and children who go for wood and eggs tomorrow. After the storm, we'll destroy this Shaitan once and for all."

Aash returned to their Gher to ask Lulu for some berries. The Gher was empty. He began asking around the village. The boys told him about the prugna, and that Lulu and Emil had left at noon. He knew that area near the river was half a day's journey. *Lulu knew about the storm. They should be well back by now.* A familiar dark shadow of fear chilled Aash's heart. He raced back to the Gher to gather weapons, and lit a torch.

Chief Sev and four hunters were waiting in blocking positions outside the Gher as he reemerged.

The Chief took a deep breath.

"Spearmaker, it's nearly sunset. We don't know where they are. The last hunting team heard the Sabretooth's roar near the river. They distinctly saw a kettle of vultures circling a kill on the horizon. The animals rule the night. It's a new moon. You can't track by pitch darkness. The storm will kill your fire. Your woman is clever, and none would wager against Emil's mind. I'm sure she and the boy are safe up in a tree. You are the People's only Spearmaker. You can't go tonight. We will send hunting teams at dawn. I'm truly sorry, Aash. This is an order. I have spoken."

Aash said, "No."

He brandished the great ivory war axe as the hunters stepped back, spreading apart. His eyes were cold fire. Sev knew firsthand the blood that ran through those veins, and how this would end. He quickly ordered the hunters back. Papa was racing out of the village as he heard the Chief shout, "We will come at dawn."

Aash found their tracks shortly before sunset. *Cloud's with them, this is good. The bad news is fresh hyena spoor on their trail. I have to hurry. A pack of hyenas is every bit as dangerous as any Sabretooth.*

The rain came as if on cue, shortly after nightfall, and mercilessly extinguished his torch. It was so dark Aash couldn't see his hand in front of his face. *This is bad.*

Lulu was holding a sleeping Emil high up in the prugna tree. They were both soaked to the bone from the storm and shivering. She knew the Sabretooth was somewhere close waiting for them. *It'd all happened in a blink.* As she'd met the great cat's charge, a savage white growling blur streaked past her. Cloud was fearless. Lulu had dropped the spear. She'd sprinted after Emil and picked him up. Lulu had heard horrible snarling sounds behind her. The dreadful lords of the forest dueled to the death with claw and fang.

Mama had just focused on getting up the tree with a wildly protesting Emil. She looked down to see the bloody Sabretooth scratching furiously at the base of the tree, seemingly mere moments after they were up high and safe.

Emil had waved his black knife angrily at the cat, screaming, "My papa will kill you!" The Sabretooth had roared back savagely, but the great cat could not reach them.

Lulu squeezed her sleeping son tighter as her thoughts flashed back to Cloud. She choked back silent tears and closed her eyes, thinking she could force this grim vision out of her mind's eye. Lulu bore sole witness to this dance of death. She had shielded Emil's eyes.

None save the Sabretooth and Cloud would ever voice their deadly contest. It was a teardrop in the infinite river of time. The white wolf's initial charge had befuddled the great cat. Cloud was lightning quick, but still a young wolf. The Sabretooth had been so focused on Lulu's charge, he'd heard rather than seen the white wolf. A more experienced wolf would have charged in silence. Instead, the cat's lightning reflexes saved him from a crippling slash to the throat. The bite was still dangerously deep.

The Sabretooth leapt forward just in time to escape Cloud's backhanded attempt to hamstring him. A flashing fast claw stroke ripped deep into Cloud's nose. Cloud yelped in pain. The white wolf's blood-splattered blue eyes briefly focused on the big tree. Then, his demeanor exuded pure fear. Cloud nearly flipped over backwards to turn around, and ran crying for the tree line.

The Sabretooth saw this weakness and fear. The primal instinct was to give chase. Cloud fled straight into a thorny deadfall. The evil cat had underestimated the white wolf's cunning once again. Thinking he'd cornered Cloud, he realized all too late, this was a superb ruse. The white wolf's position was strong. There was only space for one of them in the deadfall. Cloud's flanks and rear were now protected by thick, impenetrable thorns. The only way to attack the white wolf was to come right through his snarling teeth. The wily Sabretooth realized he'd been led further away from the hated humans. He tested the wolf, trying to lure him out with a paw feint. Cloud's response was to bite off a portion of the cat's offending paw. The Sabretooth backed off, realizing the futility of attacking the wolf in this deadfall. Cloud's eyes blazed pure insolence. He knew he was safe here, and sensed his family had time to make the tree.

The shrewd Sabretooth backed off, leering cruelly. A normal wolf would never leave this position, but this one cared for his humans. He would follow if they were in danger! The big cat spun around and charged the prugna tree with a throaty roar. Cloud sensed his family was safe, but he couldn't see from the deadfall. Had the Sabretooth seen something? Had his boy fallen from the tree? The bloody white wolf brazenly charged out after the Sabretooth.

This played right into the big cat's paws, as it whirled back on Cloud. The white wolf barely ducked a decapitating paw stroke. They circled one another slowly, growling deeply. Then the old cat noticed the young wolf held his head a bit too high. With a savage growl, he feinted at Cloud's throat and lunged low. There was a sharp crunch. The white wolf's front paw now dangled uselessly beneath him. Cloud would still not go down. He snarled defiance, hopping on his three good legs.

The Sabretooth knew it was only a matter of time for the crippled wolf. Cloud knew he couldn't win now, but he could return the favor. The white wolf slashed high in desperation for the big cat's throat—he could feint as well. Cloud felt a full paw in his mouth, and bit down through it with all his remaining strength, no matter what. The Sabretooth's jaws locked around the white fur of Cloud's neck and found the jugular. Cloud released the cat's mangled paw, making a final weak lunge for the Sabretooth's throat. The white wolf's final effort came up just short, as his lifeblood emptied from his noble throat into the trampled grass. This was Cloud, the first dog.

Emil woke up shivering in the darkness. Intermittent fireflies illuminated the Sabretooth's green eyes glowing malevolently in the darkness.

"Don't be scared, Mama, Papa will come," proclaimed Emil as he gave her a prugna. Lulu forced a grim smile. This was, in fact, exactly what Lulu was scared of despite the rain and Stygian darkness. *My sensitive little Babo is brave, and trying to comfort me. Aash will come. He'll be completely blind. The Sabretooth can see in the dark and will be waiting for him.*

False dawn found Papa restless and cursing high up an oak tree. He was doing the breathing exercise, praying to the spirits, and trying anything to keep bad visions from his mind. He lit his torch and began tracking at first light. A bit further ahead the trail had led right into a narrow bushy chapparal. A hyena clan had sheltered the night there from the storm. *The storm actually saved me. If I'd stumbled blindly upon them in the dark, they'd have torn me to pieces.*

Inexplicably, somehow the secure covers had fallen off the pair of venom darts in the quiver. He couldn't tell which two they were. Aash heard the roar of a big cat's challenge carrying over the ridge by the river. There were no answering forest sounds. Papa began sprinting and praying like a man possessed. The Sabretooth has them cornered.

Emil and Mama woke to a loud coarse scraping sound from below. The Sabretooth was back again. It let out an earsplitting roar which shook the very core of their tree. Emil screamed back, throwing his last rock at the big cat. The stone struck the blind eye of the Sabretooth, who responded with an enraged growl and slammed into the base of the tree. The impact jarred Emil's exhausted grip loose from his branch. Mama barely caught his wrist as he fell swaying from their branch. The Sabretooth reared back and sprang up high in the air. It pushed off from the trunk, barely missing Emil's dangling foot. Mama pulled with every fiber of her being. Lulu dragged her bawling son back up onto their branch, holding him close in a death grip. Her arms were spent from the cold and effort.

Mama made sure Emil was secure. She felt her own grip, frozen numb from the cold, now spent and slowly slipping from the branch. There was a brief lull in the din, as the big cat below looked up to see all of this with glee. The Sabretooth licked his chops with anticipation at what was now sure to come.

Both Lulu and Emil heard a sudden high-pitched whistling sound below. The unmistakable hearty thud of sharp flint striking solid flesh echoed loudly. The Sabretooth yelped a shrill, agonized howl and flipped on its back. It was biting with insane fervor at the dart now protruding from its haunches. Emil secured his mama back up on their branch while exclaiming, "Papa's here!"

Another venom dart thumped into the ground, just missing the big cat's head. A deep, full-throated primal battle cry boomed forth, reverberating down the thorny hillside.

"HAR HAR MAHADEV!"

The Sabretooth recovered its feet and with a quick jerk of its tail accepted the man's challenge. It gnashed its gruesome jaws and charged its tormentor with rabid guttural growls.

Papa smoothly reloaded the throwing stick with the last venom dart and took aim. Lulu and Emil both forgot to breathe, watching the low-flying tawny blur streak uphill at Papa. The last dart barely missed, scraping just high as the big cat rolled under it.

Aash took a deep breath. He knelt evenly and composedly grounded the spear butt in the earth, just as his father had taught him so long ago. In the end, Papa stood tall to meet the Sabretooth's charge with the great ivory war axe.

A charging Sabretooth will strike from low to high, unless it doesn't. It doesn't matter if you are kneeling. This ends here. No matter what.

Everything slowed down; there was no sound. Papa could see the enraged yellow eyes growing in size, ever so slowly. The cat's terrible mouth and cruel fangs ached, leaping for his throat. At the absolute very last instant, he dropped to a knee. Lulu covered Emil's eyes, with her heart in her throat.

As the great cat sprang upon him, Papa dropped the axe and pulled the heavy obsidian spear up off the ground, screaming defiance with all his strength. The impact was a sickening crunch as the big cat flipped completely head over heels, impaled. Papa was knocked back into darkness. The Sabretooth swiped a thunderous paw stroke down at the prone man as it flew over him, missing by less than a hair's width.

Papa lay dazed, waiting for the inevitable feeling of the long fangs tearing his throat. It was actually a dreamy sensation, surprisingly not unpleasant. He felt no pain. *At least it can't climb Emil's tree now*. He thought he saw the Eagle Feather. In the blur, he smiled at the thought of greeting his father once again. The deadly bite never came.

Slowly, they eventually rolled Papa to a knee. His vision was still very blurred and his balance was shaky. He stumbled for the ivory axe. There was no need. The Sabretooth was lying still in a clumping pool of dark arterial blood. The heavy ash spear shaft buried completely through the neck. Then the world went black again.

When Papa came to, he was in Mama's lap and Babo was pouring cool water on his lips. The sun shone brightly, illuminating the Eagle Feather, and Emil's smiling face from behind.

"Lulu, you changed your hair?" Papa whispered faintly as he slowly brushed the back of his bloody, broken hand down the side of her face. She started crying again.

He held Lulu's hand tightly as Emil was sobbing with happiness. "You did it, Papa! You did it! I knew it! You did it!"

Papa held them both close and tight as they gingerly helped him to his feet. His vision was clearing, but he had an awful headache. His entire left side was bruised a dark purple hue.

"Cloud and Mama saved me," gasped Emil. Papa held them both tight forever. Emil was crying again now. "It's my fault, Papa—I wanted a special prugna gift for you." Aash shook his head, not trusting his voice yet, and kissed them both again and again.

Papa's strength was returning. He sat carefully for a long time, examining the Sabretooth's carcass before skinning it. The dart had slowed the big cat. There was also another painfully deep gash straight to the bone in the Sabretooth's neck. The big cat's left front paw had been nearly bitten off. *Cloud the white wolf sold his life very dearly.* Papa realized these crippling injuries to the cat likely allowed Lulu and Emil to make it to the tree, and also slowed the cat's final charge. *I remember the fluffy, little white ball of fur Emil made us save so long ago.* Cloud the white wolf had repaid his family with the ultimate gift.

Emil and Papa locked eyes tearfully in unison. "Good."

The People's hunting team spotted them, led by more circling vultures, and roared in relief. The little family was limping silently arm in arm through a wooded clearing. The Eagle Feather visible like a shining white beacon well across the distant golden horizon.

They were pulling a hasty travois with remains of Cloud, and an enormous Sabretooth skin. Chief Sev grabbed Papa's forearm in warm greeting, then personally took a travois pole away from Mama. The hunting team escorted them home.

Papa insisted Cloud's remains be treated the same as any of the People's. By tradition, Lulu led them all in the old prayers. Mama sang a hauntingly beautiful new song for the white wolf. The Sky Spirits accepted Cloud, a straight and true member of the Auroch People.

Chapter Twenty-Three
The Eagle Feather

"An army of deer led by a lion is more to be feared than an army
of lions led by a deer."
-Greek Proverb

THE FOREST WAS SILENT that gray-lit morning. The early
morning breeze was still cool, as ripples gently flowed across
the river's shimmering surface. The hot summer sun was
tardy so far.

Aash's hunting team watched as the Mountain Men's
hollow log forded the river. Peace signs exchanged on both
sides. This was trading day. Ten pouches of salt traded for
an equal number of sable pelts and a big leather wrap of
edelweiss.

As they reached the shore there was no sign of Aki. Aash noticed, *Inga is here instead of Aki. Why is she wearing furs dyed black? What's wrong?*

Inga saw his new Sabretooth claw necklace and the freshly wrapped poultice around his left hand. Inga greeted him with a sad smile. The goods were exchanged quickly.

The Spearmaker signed, "I...thank Aki.... edelweiss...save Lulu.... here gift." He offered Inga a beautiful obsidian dagger with an ivory handle. He'd crafted it out of gratitude for the giant hunter.

Inga's face quivered. "I accept...for Mountain Men...Aki gone, Sabretooth.... five nights ago." With her hands she described in anguish how the cat had somehow torn through their hut's door as they slept. It'd dragged Aki away on a dark moonless night. She signed, "Shaitan.... drag Aki far...before kill." She pointed at Aash's necklace.

Aash sighed, signing," Yes.... the Sabretooth dead.... We kill four days ago. Without hesitation he removed the necklace, offering it to the young widow.

"Aki... avenged...you take," Aash signed.

Inga shook her head. She could never wear something she hated so deeply. She signed back, "Thank you... you save me...you avenge Aki..." Then with dignified grace she stepped back into their boat. The Mountain Men and Inga rowed back across.

On the walk back to the village Aash thought of Aki and grimaced.

Ironically, the giant's immense strength probably only increased his suffering. Why had the cat dragged him so far before killing him? What must have gone through the poor fellow's mind? He'd been dragged to his death, knowing he'd never see his loved ones again, and nothing could save him. Life is not fair; no one deserves that fate.

He remembered the tranquil, almost peaceful feeling he'd had when the Sabretooth had hit him. *I hope Aki also experienced this.* Aash silently offered up the same prayer for the Mountain Man that they used for their own fallen hunters. "Blue Skies warrior, thank you for saving my son."

Papa was crafting a new throwing stick later that day, when Emil asked to show him something.

Mama was with them and had helped the boys set up a wooden throwing target. She greeted Papa with a kiss. Lulu covered her mouth out of sympathy when he told her of Aki's fate. They held hands to the side of the boys as she mentioned, "I've been helping Emil with this for the past moon cycle. The boys have been practicing hard and wanted to surprise you."

Emil and the boys stood in tandem. They faced the wooden target at twice the range a throwing stick dart could reach. Emil had a springy, coiled, rawhide sling, with a smooth rock in a pouch. He whirled it around his head and stepped toward the target. With an overhand snapping motion, he hurled the rock at the target. The fist-sized stone zinged into the target, shattering it with a dull crunch. Then all the boys followed suit. A hailstorm of zinging rocks struck the target area with deadly velocity, and rapid subsequent salvos. Papa was amazed. *Some boys were better than others, but the barrage was deadly. The sling had twice the range and could be reloaded much faster than a throwing stick.* He imagined it would be hell to be a herd of prey animals or a line of hunters on the receiving end of these slinging rocks. *The force was incredibly powerful when it hit. These slings were truly lethal weapons.*

Emil came up to show Papa the sling.

"Papa, remember before the storm when the Gher strap broke and that rock flew so far into the trees? Mama helped me make this from old water pouches. We've been trying different lengths and stones. We practice every day. The strongest boys can sling almost three times farther than a throwing stick. We aren't accurate enough to hunt with them yet. We get better every day. Most of us can already hit a man-sized target at throwing-stick range most throws. With practice, I think this could be another big help to the People." The possibilities were endless. Papa hugged his son in genuine amazement. *The hunters all needed to see this.*

That night was a "Man Talk." Emil and Papa headed out toward the night tree near dusk. It seemed like Emil was waiting for something. As they took in the peaceful sounds of summer in the forest, Emil spoke. "I'm sorry, Papa. I just keep waiting for Cloud to catch up rushing out of some bushes. I guess it's still hard to believe he's gone."

Papa put his arm around Emil as they made their way up the hill. The waning sun highlighted his eagle feather. *At this angle, the boy looks so much like his opa.* Papa did a double-take. It was a quiet, star-filled night on the platform.

Papa noticed Emil was a bit quiet. They talked a bit about Aki, and agreed he was a good man who didn't deserve his brutal fate. Papa observed:

"Emil, like you, Aki was by nature a cheerful, happy person. I don't think this is an accident; I think it's a skill. We are pack animals at the end of the day; you can get a solid measure of a person by the kinds of people he or she surrounds themselves with. Good and bad things happen to all of us. You need to find excuses to be happy in life instead, of angry or sad. This sounds obvious and easy. I learned this habit is up to you, regardless of your circumstances. It's equally important to, as best you can, surround yourself with likeminded people. Those who are actively trying to be happy and healthy themselves. In fact, I actually ask myself this blunt question: is this a person looking for excuses to be happy? The answer tells me a great deal."

Papa could tell this didn't seem like an earth-shattering observation for Emil, who was by nature always cheerful and smiling. *I hope this never changes, son. This is a powerful gift.*

Emil was mainly focused on Lupus. Papa could tell he was wondering if the white wolf had taken his place high up in the heavens with the Sky Spirits watching over the People.

"I wish Cloud had been made of rock so the Sabretooth couldn't have hurt him," Emil remarked.

Papa responded.

"Yes, but then he wouldn't have been that fluffy little ball of fur we saved that day. Cloud showed what he was made of whenever things got tough. I know what you mean though. Your mama and I will always see you as our baby. We wish you were made of obsidian, so nothing could ever hurt you either. But that wouldn't be our Emil. Our vulnerabilities and weaknesses are part of what makes us who we are. If you truly love someone, you learn this. Life is hard, but that's also what makes it so beautiful—we are all unique and mortal. There will never be another day just like this. There will never be another person like you, or your loved ones. Learn to cherish the vulnerability, fragility, and beauty of as many days as you are given. Emil, you are everything your mother and I could ever have dreamed of in a son. We love you, are proud of you, and this will never change."

Dawn found them still cuddled up in the tree.

They awoke to an acrid smell of smoke in the air. The panicked thrashing of herd animals fleeing a forest fire came from the north. Papa gauged the winds as Emil coughed from the smoke.

Papa observed, "The fire is high up in the north hills. Unless the winds shift completely, I think the village will be safe. We need to get out of here though. Let's stay close since we'll have to pass closer than I'd like to get home."

The cackling of the flames was a dull, faraway roar, but another bass sound was echoing through the smoky air. Papa strained his ears and closed his eyes to concentrate. *It was the Auroch horns of the People!* The horns were only sounded in emergency. They called for all the People to return at once. Emil had seen the great horns but rarely heard them sound.

"Papa, are those the Auroch horns?" Emil wondered.

Papa nodded and led his son rapidly downhill on the game trail. They were making a very good pace, when Papa noticed Emil had stopped. He turned to implore his son to move fast. *The fire isn't far behind us.* Emil put a finger to his nose and pointed to a thorny berry bush just where the trail suddenly dropped off. Papa ran back to grab Emil's arm. His son cupped one hand over his ear, and pointed into the bushes.

Then Papa heard the unmistakable whimpers of newborn wolf cubs. The parents were nowhere to be seen and a full litter of five fluffy, crying cubs were alone in the bush. Papa's head was on a swivel looking for the pack. It was clear they had been lost in panic, or swept up by the smoke. He guessed the wolves had carried away as many as they could. *The fire is coming fast.*

When Emil and Papa came coughing into the village, there were dazed expressions on the People's faces. At first, they thought it was because of the new wolf cubs they were carrying. It wasn't. Papa could see now the village was in no danger from the fires. So, what was it?

Mama greeted them both with a big hug and was gushing at the little pups. She took two in her arms from Emil and whispered something in Papa's ear. Aash nodded slowly, and handed over the remaining cubs to Emil and Mama. He headed briskly for the Chief's Gher.

The village Elders were waiting for Papa in the large Gher. Chief Sev had passed peacefully in the night.

The Elders greeted Papa warmly and had closed the Chief's eyes. Papa looked down, thinking it was as serene as he'd ever seen the Chief's weathered face. The Elders placed their hands on Papa's shoulders. "You will lead the People now as per Sev's decision, until the Eagle Feather passes the trials of manhood."

Papa shook his head. "I'm honored, but there are other men who want this. Men who would do a much better job. I just want to make spears, and raise my boy with Lulu."

The Chief Elder declared:

"Sev predicted you would say this almost verbatim. He proclaimed this is exactly why you must be Chief, until Emil is ready. Life is hard for the People. The fact you don't want the power, makes you exactly the right man. The best way for you to serve your family is to lead the People with strength and compassion. Your father and Sev have done so before you. It must be you. Emil will still not be told of his future, but frankly we'd be shocked if the boy hasn't already figured this out. We will announce this at the evening meal."

Papa opened the flap of their Gher to a warm greeting from Mama and the sight of Emil playing with a tiny, but feisty brown wolf cub. His son was ecstatic with laughter again.

"He was the runt of the litter, but the feistiest!" laughed Emil, "He reminds me of Bret, so I chose him. I'm going to call him Bear!"

The evening meal that night started out a bit quieter than usual. The People were surprised and chastened by the passing of Chief Sev. However, the Elders' decision had unanimous support. Sev had given strict final orders the People were to eat, drink, and dance in his absence! They did so in memory of the gruff, thoughtful old warrior, who'd led them with such wisdom.

Aash was made Chief of the Auroch People in a quiet ceremony at dawn. The Elders anointed his temples with the sacred ochre paints. He raised the obsidian-tipped ivory war staff held by the Auroch Chief. *It somehow seemed much heavier than yesterday*, he thought.

The Spirit Ceremony for Chief Sev was held that afternoon. Emil's papa, Chief Aash of the Auroch People, addressed his subjects for the first time.

"My brothers and sisters, you honor me with the ivory staff. Life is hard, but beautiful. None of us expected this. I'm wondering if this staff means now my son will listen and go to bed when asked. We will see. However, there are things I know. The man lying in front of us was a true blessing to the People. His strength and wisdom allowed us to prosper. Sev was born in a time of war. A fate many of us here have luckily never known. Sev was proud of this. If you look at this man's body, it bears the scars of a lifetime of service to the People. It should come to no surprise that all of his battle scars are on the front of his body.

"Those of us who served with him know what he'd say if he could hear us now. Sev would say, 'It's because I could run really fast!' I only ever saw him move one way, and that was for the heart of the danger. Sev taught me two things. The first is freedom isn't free. Only strength and diligence protect our happiness. Second, discipline is freedom. We are a resourceful, resilient people, and our ancestors watch over us. We will be strong, we will be compassionate, we will be free.

"Sky Spirits, accept Chief Sev. A true and straight hunter, soar into the heavens of our ancestors."

With this final salute, the pyres were lit.

The new Chief addressed the People at the evening meal later that day.

"We have some developments and changes.

"First, we have found a litter of new wolf cubs. They will be trained as Cloud was to help hunt, and protect the People. Emil will be responsible for this training in addition to his existing duties. Each of the pups has his own family. I believe they can be trained to run down game for us and help defend the People if needed.

"Second, we need a new Spearmaker, actually two. I will train anyone interested. There is no reason this post cannot go to a woman. This would free up another hunter.

"Third, and this is high priority, the hunting teams will remain intact for the most part. I want all the hunters to focus on the new sling weapon the boys have developed. It will amaze you. The hunters are first priority, but the women and the girls must also be taught the sling for defense. Finally, we are a proud people and honor our heritage. This will never change.

"Think, my friends, on the changes in our lives over the past few winters. We have throwing sticks, slings, poison darts, and a Falling Spear mammoth trap. Wolves now hunt and fight for us. We can smoke meat now that lasts a full winter. We have snowshoes to run in heavy powder and better hunting in sectors. We have edelweiss and warmer furs, from trade with the Mountain Men. All of this and more. We must remain diligent, for our territory is rich in game, yet we trade with our neighbors instead of just killing one another. We also survived the evils of the Sabretooth. All of this was possible because of imagination, courage, and keeping our minds open. If you have an idea that may help the People, share it! Don't be afraid."

Dawn found a tanned boy's feisty brown wolf cub merrily fetching a thrown stick. He had a brilliant white Eagle Feather in his hair, and an obsidian black knife hung on his hip. A throwing stick and dart quiver were slung over his shoulder. There was a sling and rock pouch on his belt. Papa and Emil always went first, to check the ground for snakes.

The boys of the Auroch People led their cubs into the silver-brown savannah for morning puppy training. Mama and Papa smiled. They could hear the excited barks of the cubs mixed with the laugher of the little ones.

A falcon's shrill call caught their attention, as he dove from the heavens onto a fleeing pigeon. Emil replayed the bird strike in his mind's eye and ran over to his parents. It seemed a single white puffy cloud was lingering overhead, just for him. Emil smiled at this.

"Papa, Papa, Papa, I got an idea—did you see how fast and straight that falcon flew when it dove? What if we attached feathers to the back of the darts—they should fly better! Right?"

The flashing white Eagle Feather danced in the young amber sunlight.

Life is hard, but beautiful.

Food for Thought for Young People

1.   What's the idea behind making your bed first thing every morning, and being early?

2.   Why are strength and compassion equally important in life?

3.   What's the value of telling the truth in the nicest way?

4.   What does it mean to avoid the second mistake?

5.   How can dark humor help tough situations?

6.   What does it mean that the only thing you can control in life is believing in yourself? Is this true? How much of life is luck?

7.   What does the question "Is this virtue or vanity" mean?

8.   Is bravery doing ordinary things in extraordinary circumstances?

9.	What is the philosophy behind saying "Good" to adversity?

10.	What does "Do good without expectation" mean?

Find Me on Socials

Did you enjoy The Eagle Feather?

Would it be crazy to ask for a one or two line review?

It's so helpful for an Indie Author.

What did you think about the story?

__ It was great, write more books!

__ It beat a sharp poke in the eye

__ Don't quit your day job

__ Go pound sand!

I'D LOVE TO HEAR from you at akvyas.com! "Wooden Nickels" is the free monthly A.K. Vyas books monthly newsletter!I'd like to invite you to join **"Wooden Nickels,"** my monthly newsletter! There are book extras, writing tips, contents, prizes, food for thought and the odd irresistible Tex-Mex recipe. It's also where I often seek your input on covers, character names, book titles, etc., and my list for new releases, special sales, and giveaways. **Join the fun.**

Website: akvyas.com

Facebook: @akvbook

Twitter: @akvyas18

Instagram: @akvyasauthor

What's Next in the Series?
Winter's Wind

Several winters have passed since the events of The Eagle Feather. Emil, and the young Auroch boys are now on the cusp of the Trials of Manhood. The ancient rite of passage requires proof of survival skills in a savage, frigid, desolate wilderness. The boys must leave their People. If they survive, they earn the right to return home as men of their tribe.

However, the chilling Winter's Winds have spurred something wicked in the world. An ancient merciless evil, has returned to Auroch Lands.

Life is still Beautiful, but it's about to get a lot harder...

ACKNOWLEDGEMENTS

No man goes through life, or writes a book without a great deal of help. I'm sincerely humbled by the efforts of those who saw fit to believe in this project. I'm eternally grateful to my family and friends on both sides of the Atlantic. Texas, Missouri, New York, California, London, and now Germany are all home for me. Everything starts and ends with all of you. When you are loved, all things are possible.

I would especially like to thank Andrew, Jayanth, and Rob. Last and certainly not least, The Eagle Feather would simply not have been possible without the steadfast support of Danny King, and the keen eye of a local artist, Ms. Fatima Sabra.

Finally, if possible, I'd like to express gratitude for experiencing the unique entrepreneurial spirit of the San Francisco Bay Area. It's an exceptional region where young people truly believe they can change the world.

About the Author

A.K. Vyas gave early promise of being nothing special whatsoever. He was born in the small New England village best known for the witch trials, then banished to Texas at a tender age. Being annoyingly well-read for a Texan and exceptionally stubborn as a child, the smart money predicted a brief but clumsy career as a rodeo clown, while others foresaw an early death.

To everyone's intense disbelief, UC Berkeley made the mistake of admitting him, and he squeaked out a degree or two while doing silly acrobatic things in small planes. The Navy eventually decided it was safer for all parties involved if he didn't fly jets. Like most wayward souls he ended up on Wall Street, a lifestyle interrupted from time to time by an occasional date, unless of course it was NCAA football season. (You can take a boy out of Texas, but you can't take Texas out of the boy.)

To date, his young family has survived two Category 5 hurricanes, and an infatuation with TexMex cast-iron skillet recipes. Europe is currently home, and for unknown reasons, people on the street everywhere always ask him for directions. The Eagle Feather is his debut attempt at the ancient art of storytelling, and was written for his beautiful, perfect, athletic, and wonderful son.

ALSO BY A.K. VYAS

Ballad of Shannon Dumas Series

Shannon is a frontier tale set amidst the backwoods bayous of antebellum Louisiana, the sprawling decadence of old New Orleans, and the mercilessly rugged Texas frontier.

Texas Tales

Texas Tales is a series of Western short stories about the legendary wanderings of a lone cowboy you'll root for on the 19th Century Texas Frontier.

Carnival Girls

Carnival Girls is a dark international thriller about a chilling serial killer who abducts coeds and the FBI agent trying to bring him to justice.

www.ingramcontent.com/pod-product-compliance
Lightning Source LLC
Chambersburg PA
CBHW032225050726
47591CB00001B/260